# WHO'S
# WHO

*enjoy !!* :)

# WHO'S WHO

## SUSAN KAY BOX BRUNNER

*Susan Kay Box Brunner*

TATE PUBLISHING
AND ENTERPRISES, LLC

Published by Tate Publishing & Enterprises, LLC
127 E. Trade Center Terrace | Mustang, Oklahoma 73064 USA
1.888.361.9473 | www.tatepublishing.com

Tate Publishing is committed to excellence in the publishing industry. The company reflects the philosophy established by the founders, based on Psalm 68:11,
*"The Lord gave the word and great was the company of those who published it."*

Book design copyright © 2016 by Tate Publishing, LLC. All rights reserved.
*Cover design by Joshua Rafols*
*Interior design by Shieldon Alcasid*

Published in the United States of America

ISBN: 978-1-68333-087-5
Fiction / Christian / Romance
16.06.03

Susan Kay Box Brunner,
the author, wishes to thank the following people:
Larry Brunner, the encourager and listener's ear;
Dustin Lewis, photographer;
Donna Stephens, sharing information
on Satish Adhem, the Arabian Horse.

# Chapter 1

THEODOR WELCH CAME into the office at 3:00 a.m. straight from the airport to play catch-up with his e-mails. After several strong cups of coffee and several hours later, his clients would be pleased when they open their e-mails to see their returns from all their investments.

The office phones began ringing off the hook. He grabbed the line and hurriedly jotted down notes and continued from one phone call after another. By midmorning, more updates and e-mails were sent and recorded. He stood and entwined his fingers and stretched out his arms and yawned. "Man, I'm lucky Ms. Cheryl Tally works here. She's reliable and a one-of-a-kind receptionist. She's a whiz at keeping up and answering our daily phone calls." He listened and noticed his phone line was not lit up.

Theodor glanced at the desk calendar, letting out a breath. "This workload is just too much for me to handle anymore." He sat down and made a note for Miss Tally, "I needed a dedicated, full-time, younger assistant, who is hungry for his or her foot to succeed in the world of financial investment advisory." Then said, "Now all I need is to convince Miss Tally on this matter." He shuddered. "A blessing and a curse, my clients have tripled in the last six months, again this year, and I have another early morning departure. Destination, Mexico." He refocused and continued sending out e-mails to his clients, updating them of their financial investment status. Theodor searched the files for anyone who had given referrals to make sure he had notified them.

Theodor closed his eyes for a moment and thought, *My king-size bed is calling me.* He shook his head and flipped back through the calendar, checking off places where he had spoken for the Edwin Jays National Investments Conference. *Spain, and the previous month, in Turkey, and Bolivia.* He sighed, "Life is so hectic. I've worked and pushed hard for the last seventeen years to top position as the 'International Financial Advisor.'" Rubbing the back of his neck, he continued, "Even as a young lad, my father lectured me to use my math smarts, and his expectations ran high." He glanced out in his office, "I wish he was alive to see my accomplishments and enjoy a wealthy retirement life." He stretched again. "So you love work and that means travel."

Suddenly, Theodor's smartphone vibrated. Chuckling, he said, "Must be one of the women Miss Tally didn't allow through on the main line." She had just marched into his office tsk-tsking and tossing fifteen messages from two women he escorted around town whenever the need arose. Pinching his nose, he pulled out his cell phone. The name Tara Scott was registered. Drum rolling his fingers on his massive mahogany desk, he asked, "Who is Tara Scott?" He reached for the local phone line and pushed the call button.

"Yes, Mr. Welch."

"Miss Tally, come into my office!"

Within seconds, old spinster Miss Tally appeared inside his office doorway, wearing oversized white-rimmed glasses, which set on the tip of her nose. She was verily five foot tall even in her two-inch Dr. Scholl's pump shoes. He muffled a chuckle with a cough, arching his nearly perfect back brows. "Miss Tally, Do you recall a client by the name of Tara Scott?"

Her thin red lipstick lips disappeared while staring back at her boss. "No, sir. That name doesn't ring a bell. Why?"

Theodore ran a hand through his well-kept jet-back hair. "I received a text message to meet a Tara Scott at the 'Marcello Restaurant' tonight six p.m." He stood and pointed at the calendar. "She's not scheduled, and I've thumbed through the last three month's e-mails and there's nothing. So, Miss Tally, check all our boxed files dating back six months and send me the required information on her."

Miss Tally nodded and turned closing his office door.

Theodor finished his daily inputs and looked at his Maurice Lacroix watch, now 4:15 p.m. "If I leave now, I can be home and back within the hour." Theodor straightened his silk tie and pushed the landline call button again.

"Yes, Mr. Welch?"

"Anything on Tara Scott, Miss Tally?"

She sighed. "No! I would have sent you the information. However, I'm still looking."

"All right. I'm leaving the office for the day. Hopefully you'll find information on Tara Scott. Oh, Miss Tally, hold my calls from Elisha, Jeannette, and Georgina. Tell them I'm out of town or at a conference."

"Tsk-tsk, Mr. Welch. You and your wondering bachelor ways are going to be the death of me yet."

"Now, Miss Tally." He counted to five letting her comment go, then said, "If I hurry across town, I'll pack for my trip to Mexico, shower, and still be able to meet this mysterious woman. I'll e-mail you from Mexico or call me if I'm needed." He disconnected the phone call and passed her while breezing out of his building. Time: 5:45 p.m. He parked in front the Marcello Restaurant and said, "My old childhood neighborhood appears to be the same." He glanced farther down the street, recognizing the alley where he lived with his father. "Those were some stressful times, and humbling." Sighing, he recalled his mother's battle with phenomena and death, and that his father worked two and sometimes three jobs to make ends meet or maybe it was to hide his loneliness. He glanced at his smartphone and still no word sent by Miss Tally. He still had five minutes to kill before entering the restaurant. He took one more fleeting look up and down the street, it was quiet, no cars, no buses, not even people out walking, or a barking dog.

Theodor opened the restaurant door and inhaled the same delicious homemade smells filtering under his nose. He sauntered over to the bar and, with confidence, ordered,

"Coffee, black." Moments later, he turned around on the stool, eyeing the room, and noticed men and women seated at the tables, some were in deep conversation, or eating. Glancing to his right, three women sat alone and not a thing triggered in his mind as to which one was Tara Scott.

Theodor turned his back to the women in hopes Tara Scott would notice him and walk to the bar. He glanced at his smartphone and still no word from Miss Tally. He lifted the hot cup of coffee and sipped. Straightening his shoulders, he turned slightly again. "Man up, Theodor Welch, you've got this." He stood and began walking toward the women. Three steps in, table number 1, a rushed man slid into a seat and handed the woman flowers and very loudly apologized for his lateness. Next table—what? His large black eyes narrowed, glancing around. He saw the other tables were now empty.

Outside, he breathed in and said, "Tara Scott must not have recognized me either. Perhaps she's a friend of a client." He jammed his hands in his pockets and walked to his parked black BMW and aired, "Maybe I should have replied to her text."

Driving to the airport. "Clients will have to wait until I'm back from Mexico. And maybe Miss Tally will have the information on Tara Scott."

Theodor found Mexico City an interesting place, streets were filled with tents and people selling dry goods, beans, fish, chickens

alive and dressed, cotton clothing, straw hats, flower groupings, to name a few. However, he was in hot pursuit of meeting men and women wanting financial advice and how to invest. The need for him to stay in Mexico several extra days amazed him. He e-mailed Miss Tally of the decision and informed her to change his flight. Also asked had she advertized for another financial advisor to join forces with his company.

Miss Tally was a trusted soul. She should have already retired. He recalled their first meeting. Right after college, he swaggered into a local Edwin Jay's Investment Company and discovered that the proprietor was retiring due to health issues. Theodor Welch convinced the owner to take a chance on him and to turn the business over to Theodor after three years service as payment. The owner agreed, and Miss Tally, then sixty-two, offered to stay on until he was settled. Shaking his head. *My how the years have flown by.* Then he sent another e-mail. "Find anything on Tara Scott?"

Theodor's seminar was successful. He added forty-five new clients in Mexico. Finally, he was on a flight home to Columbus, Ohio, and thought, *I'm glad my business building is located in the capital, where there's always change, new high risers, key parking lots, new shops, gallery hops among the constant nightlife.* He rested his head feeling somewhat drained. Where was his joy in making the deals or the old excitement in adventure, or travel? He let out a breath, "It's just jet leg and hopefully not a flu bug." But a disturbing void stirred within his being.

Theodor tapped his watch. "It's only five in the evening." He drove to his office building and parked at the curb. Inside he discovered 223 unanswered e-mails that needed immediate answers. He removed his jacket, tie, and unbuttoned his top two shirt buttons and rolled up his sleeves. An hour later, now 6:00 p.m., he sent a text to Tara Scott, "Met me at Marcello Restaurant in an hour, seven p.m. I'm in from business, Mexico." He continued working for another half hour then grabbed a five-minute shower in his office suite's private bathroom. Reaching for his Aramis Cologne, he hesitated and said, "This is what I use when I date and this is no date!" He slapped on the cologne anyway.

Outside the restaurant in his BMW, he looked up and down the street finding no one. He entered the restaurant and found just a few men were sitting at the bar and to his left, women were at two different tables. He walked to the bar, ordered his usual black coffee, stayed, and watched. Men arrived within seconds and approached the women's table. He sipped the last drop. Looking at his watch, it was now seven thirty. Inside his BMW, he pounded the wheel and called Elisha Devin on speed dial.

On first ring, she huskily said, "Ted, need company?"

He grunted, "Be at your place in fifteen minutes."

"Waiting." She giggled.

He knocked on her door. She greeted him with a full-on-the-mouth kiss and pulled him through the door. He knew the hot-blooded model, Elisha, liked being seen on his arm at high society events. And sometimes they enjoyed a private moment or two. They had an understanding of no strings attach. Both were out for only a good time.

She loosened the tie and reached the buttons on his shirt. One by one were quickly opened; then she jerked his shirt off. He kissed her back and suddenly lifted his head—nothing, no sparks, but there'd never been any electricity. Theodor stepped back and raised his hands. "Sorry, Elisha, But I've made a huge mistake tonight." He grabbed his shirt and keys and opened her high-rise condo door. He slid into his shirt, and he heard something hit the door. She was screeching out a foreign language. Shaking his head, he chuckled. Sitting behind the wheel of his BMW, he thought, *I've always been a passionate soul and able to perform automatically since I was fifteen years old.* Theodor reached his cell phone and hit the steering wheel. A text from Tara Scott. "Just got your message, alright, running late." He saw the time was now eight thirty. He hurried to the restaurant and pulled up in front as the owner locked the door. What could he to do now? Send Tara Scott flowers? He didn't have an address. What a hot mess. He blew out a held breath. Theodor made a U-turn and at his gated townhouse, entered, and said, "I need to man up and call Tara Scott, and what?"

Looking at the time, it was now 9:45 p.m. Too late to make a first-time business call. Instead, Theodor took a long cold shower and let the water cascade over him. He felt exhausted, muscles ached, but sleep avoided him. He thought, *First thing in the morning, I'll talk with Miss Tally and find out if there was any response to the ad placed for a financial advisor and if she found anything on Tara Scott.*

The sun was blinding, he had fallen asleep. Theodor grabbed his pounding head. Time: 7:00 a.m. He hurriedly dressed, shaved, got in the BMW, and all but ran into the building. In passing Miss Tally, he said, "Come into my office—now!"

She entered his office, closed the door, and turned while still pointing her wrinkled index finger. He opened his mouth when she reached his ear and pulled it. "Theodor Welch, you sit there and listen up. My name is not jump, skip, or hop!" Her large white-rimmed glasses scooted further down her nose. "I know my job, but what about you and this flyby night almost happening at Elisha's? You said, quote, 'Tell her I'm not available.' Tsk-tsk, the phone has done nothing but ring off the hook from that woman!" She raised a wrinkled hand and said, "Don't talk." She shoved noted phone calls from Elisha Devin in front of him. "Theodor, you need to grow up and change your worldly ways. Find a real woman. One that's wholesome." Her stare nailed him to his seat. "Yes, I placed the ad for a financial advisor and asked for a reply by fax into the office by Thursday twelve noon. I double-checked your schedule, and you're in town free until Friday morning. Now about Tara Scott." She handed him several paper printouts.

He glanced at the papers.

"We have nothing on her. But after searching the Internet, I found three women, name, Tara Scott. One is as old as I am though. So that leaves two possibilities. Familiarize yourself with their looks so if you meet, you'll know who's who." She marched to the door, opened it, and paused. "Theodor, stay away from those painted up rail-thin women. You'll be thirty-seven in two days." Miss Tally tsk-tsked, shaking her head, walking toward her desk.

Theodor rubbed his chin. "I need to stay on Miss Tally's good side." He worked on correspondence for a while then pulled out his smartphone and called Tara Scott. It went straight to voice mail. He cleared his throat and left a message, "Sorry we keep missing one another, however, let's meet at the Marcello Restaurant say six thirty tonight, on the outside of the restaurant. Thank you." He hung up and slid his smartphone in his pocket and instantly remembered he didn't give his business title or name. "I'm not calling back." Seconds later, straight to voice mail again. "I left an earlier message. I'm Theodor Welch." He ended the call. "You dumb, dumb."

He continued working until 5:00 pm. He used his office suite's private bathroom and showered, changing into his spare clothes. Theodor addressed a note to Miss Tally, requesting his suit and dress shirt be sent to the cleaners. He slipped on his Captor shoes and checked himself in the mirror, smiling at his own reflection. "I'm a good-looking fellow. Solid, muscular, hum"—opening his mouth—"straight white teeth, and my height, six foot three, just like my father. I'm a man's man." He jelled his hair into the new tousled style and touched the silvering beginning at his temples. "Just like my father's." Straightening, he stretched and rolled out his shoulders, leaving the office with Miss Tally's care note and clothes.

He punched in a number to the local florist and ordered Miss Tally a blue orchid for blue was her favorite color. He could hear Miss Tally now telling him about his reckless spending, but he knew secretly she would love the thought. He chuckled. He slid from the parked BMW and waited in front of the restaurant. Out of habit, he glanced at his watch, 6:35 p.m. Theodor gazed up and down the street and suddenly someone touched his arm. Immediately over his shoulder, he gazed down at the most wholesome, breathtaking woman he had ever seen. She had an hourglass figure, long shoulder-length wavy bright-red hair with the most piercing sky-blue eyes. He felt electricity snap. What a lovely vision in a yellow flower sundress midthigh, little makeup, little lip gloss, and black mascara. Thinking, *She has to be in her late twenties early thirties, but she looks like a teenager.* His lips uplift. "Tara Scott?"

She only nodded.

"I'm Theodor Welch. If you don't mind, there's a nice coffee shop down the street a little ways."

Again she nodded and smiled.

Theodor placed his large hand on the small of her back, guiding her. He felt the same tingle of current ran through the length of his body. At the coffee shop, he opened the door and directed her to a tall round table, holding her seat. "What's your flavor?"

"Medium size mocha latte. Hold the whip cream."

He smiled and moved toward the counter, blowing out a held breath. Theodor saw the opposite side of the room in the long wall mirror. He spotted Tara, and she was eyeing him from head to toe and back. He caught her sparkling blue eyes, and they widened. He deepened his smile and winked. Carrying their coffee order, he observed her face, and it was still pink. He handed her the mocha latte. Their fingers met briefly, and he notice she pulled back her hand and quickly placed them in her lap. Had she felt something?

Theodor began, "I think introductions would be proper. I'm a local financial advisor, and I own a building at Main and High Street called 'Welch, Edwin Jay's Investments,' known worldwide. My first name is Theodor."

She held up her cup and took a sip of her latté. "Thank you." She did not meet his eyes.

He followed suit and sipped his black coffee and waited for her to speak. He thought, *My, I like her yellow sundress, and she's shy.* He made mention of his world travels and speaking engagements then stopped.

Her smile met her ocean-blue eyes.

*My, her lips are tempting.* Theodor spoke inwardly, "Get under control, Theodor. She's not your date, but a possible client." He cleared his throat. "Tara Scott, is that a Miss or Mrs? And how may I service you?"

Tara's neck to face reddened. She excused herself.

He stood and nodded and thought, *What did I say? What is she thinking? I'm clueless.* He reordered a black coffee and her mocha latte, hold the whip cream.

# Chapter 2

TARA RETURNED TO the table with her hands not quite folded in her lap.

"Shall we reschedule our meeting, Miss Scott? I know the hour is getting late."

Tara felt ill and somewhat faint, but willed herself to focus and urgently spoke, "I'm sorry, but would you have my mocha latte placed in a to-go cup. I need to leave." She stood.

With narrowed black eyes, he walked to the counter and retrieved a carryout cup and held the cup while she poured in the latte. Tara said, "Um, thank you and yes, I would like for us to meet again, but I really must hurry. The last bus runs in just eight minutes."

He blinked and found himself saying, "I'll drop you off at your place."

She was blushing again. She nodded no. "The bus is fine."

Theodor didn't know why he felt so protective of her, but she was not going to ride a bus in the dark not at 10:00 p.m. Where had the time gone? He placed his hand on the middle of her back, opened the coffee shop door, and said, "I'll take you home." His lips twitched. "After all, I've missed several meetings with you." The bus went by.

She slid into his BMW, and he closed her door. She thought, *Such a breathtaking gentleman.*

He came around and sat behind the wheel of his car and said, "Where to?"

"It's a ways."

He shrugged his shoulders.

She stared at him then said, "5542 White Road that's in Grove City 43123 zip code." She didn't see a muscle on him twitch. His smile remained.

He set his map guide on his smartphone and headed south. She fought with herself.

She needed to explain to Theodor Welch that he was not the man she thought she had texted. But her tongue seemed to be stuck to the roof of her mouth. She used the headrest and became deep in thought. *The man from the dating site name was Timothy something? How had I texted in the wrong number? I wished Theodor was Timothy. Wow, what a handsome man.* She peeked from one eye, looking at his presence, his stature, his kind face.

Warmth touched her arm. She shivered. Where was she? Tara looked up. "Oh, did you say something?"

He glanced her way. "Yes, and when would you like us to meet again?"

She sat forward with a hand on the door handle. "We're here." Tara leaned over and brushed a light kiss on his warm cheek. She slid from his car and let the door shut. She ran to her front door, fumbled with the key, tried again, and finally opened the door. She let out a held breath and leaned against the bolted structure. *Why did I kiss him?* Shakily, she texted Theodor, "I'm available Thursday evening at six p.m." Tara dropped her things and said, "I'll tell Mr. Welch in person so he'll understand my mishap in texting and maybe he'll get a laugh!"

She lifted a vinyl strip on the closed blind. Theodor's BMW was pulling away. She watched until the red taillights were out of sight. Suddenly, she was surrounded by her oversized Saint Bernard, which begged to be petted. She heard the chattering guinea pigs. She shook her head. The shelter was over their capacity in animals. And knowing the shelter's adoption party for all the dogs, cats, and guinea pigs was held in a few days, Tara rescued the small extra critters on a temporary assignment. After all, the Scott's Animal Shelter was her life. She had used most of her inheritance monies from her family's life insurance policy to buy the land and have the shelter built. Helping animals was a born passion.

It was pass their feeding time. Snow the Saint Bernard, who was mostly white and had a tail of blotchy gray, whined to go into the backyard. Her stomach also growled. She opened the back door, and Snow rushed past her, woofing and sniffing the air. She measured vitamins into a pail of cool water and began dipping the guinea pigs sterilized water bottles into the pail. Forty-five minutes later, ten little adorable furry and straight-haired, different-colored guinea pigs were now watered and feed.

She heard the scratch on the back door. Tara laughed. "Coming, Snow." She opened the door, and Snow rushed past her and slid to his feed bowl. "Snow, you're next." She dipped into the balance Purintia Dog Food Mix and placed two cups of dried food in Snow's bowl. She scratched his head and then added cool tap water to the gallon water bowl.

It was past midnight. Her stomach rumbled, reminding her again she hadn't ate. Opening the refrigerator door, she pulled out lunch meat, lettuce, and tomato. Tara reached for the bread and piled the meat high. She flipped out the lights and sat in the living room chair and flopped her feet on the ottoman, finishing her sandwich in the dark. Her eyes fluttered. She rested her head and promised to go to bed soon. Tara's mind drifted. *Theodor Welch was all man with those piercing black eyes. He was tall, broad shoulders, and attentive to detail and dressed expensively. And oh, his black laid-out BMW. He also owned a company. He was way out of her league.* She awoke startled. Snow laid his large head in her lap.

"Okay, boy, let's go to bed." Tara shuffled into the bathroom and, out of habit, showered and wished secretively that Theodor

Welch would join her. She lathered up again and said, "Snap out of this line of thinking. You need to pray a lot." She yawned. "He thinks I'm a business client!" She thought, *Maybe he's married although I couldn't recall a wedding band.* "No, his left ring finger was defiantly bare. No more thoughts on him."

Tara plumped her pillow and adjusted the covers. She glanced at the alarm clock, pulled out the ringer, and set the time for 6:00 a.m. Snow snuggled by her feet, and she nudged him over and slept.

The clock shook from the piercing sound. Tara slammed the ringer off and jumped from bed. In fifteen minutes, she was dressed. She grabbed her purse, keys, and said, as if the dog understood, "Watch the house, Snow."

The dog's tail moved back and forth. The door closed. She ran two blocks and whistled. The bus stopped, and the driver recognized her. She rode for two and a half miles and got off at her work, Scott Animal Shelter on Strington Road. She smiled and said, "Right on time, seven a.m." She opened the door and switched on the overhead lights and entered the security code. After her, Mary Beth, a college girl, came in and positioned her body behind the front desk. Tara headed for the clinic in the rear, switching on the overhead lights, and heard her traveling veterinarian uncle come in through the back door.

"Hi, my favorite niece," her uncle said.

"Hello, Uncle Doug. I see you finally made it. Is the area I selected for your tiny house all right?"

He shrugged and said, using his cowboy dialogue, "Slow down, Tara, the spot by the ravine is right on. But already I'm itching to be back on the road."

"Uncle Doug, you promised me three months of your time. That's what it will take for me to have my veterinarian license."

He huffed, "I always keep my promises." Hands on hips. "Tara, where does a guy go for fun around here? Like a man's place to hang out?"

Just then, the door to the clinic opened, and a dog carried by a crying woman entered.

The receptionist was walking fast on the heels of the distraught woman. Tara turned, but her uncle stepped forward and motioned for the woman to lay her dog on the long table. "Say, what's your pup's name?" he asked.

"Butch," the woman said.

"And your name?"

"Jill Price."

"Well, Ms. Price."

"No, no"—shaking her head—"it's just miss. Call me Jill."

"All right Jill"—his smile deepened—"tell me what happened to Butch."

"He was chasing squirrels and darted out into the street." She started sobbing.

Doug motioned to Tara to take the crying woman out into the waiting room. The receptionist followed, tapping the board of the unsigned consent form.

Doug observed the dog and spoke, "Broken leg, fixable. Cut over left eye, need stitches. Possible stay overnight."

Tara returned and looked down at the dog. "Well?"

"Did Miss Price give written permission to operate on Butch?"

Tara nodded and watched while he placed on the white lab coat, scrubbed his hands, and barked out, "I want number 2 needle and tape, two pop cycle sticks, don't forget the antiseptic." He sprinkled baby powder in his gloves and snapped them on.

Watching Doug was both educational and fascinating. What a natural. Tara was so proud of her uncle. He worked on cattle/horse farms across the states for nearly forty-five years. Some called him a horse whisperer. He still wore cowboy boots and a Stetson cowboy hat. Although in his midsixties, he was muscular like a bull and was naturally tanned by the sun. She was glad he had stayed in touch with her especially after her parent's death. She recalled a few months back he'd called and said, "Tara, I retired from ranching, punching cows, and breaking horses." He laughed. "Can you believe I've bought me a tiny house? I can travel wherever and live off the land, maybe even get me a dog."

That day, she asked Doug to fill in as a temporary veterinarian at her clinic. She explained she would be taking the state board veterinarian test soon and should be licensed within three months.

Tara heard yawning sounds in the background and noticed Butch seemed hypnotized. It appeared her uncle Doug was also a dog whisperer. He moved his fingers quickly and set the dog's leg. Then he checked the eye area and used only five stitches. She helped rinse the blood from the animal, and Doug carefully towel blotted the areas. He counted to three, snapped his fingers, and Butch barked. He reached for a pill relaxer and massaged Butch's throat then carried a zoned out Butch to a large cage where the dog would be secured and sleep. He washed and sterilized his hands, gloved up again, then turned his attention on a cat who needed eyedrops place in the feline's allergic eyes. He stopped after cleanup and caught up Butch's and the cat's paperwork before changing lab coat, scrubbing hands, and snapping on gloves again. He moved on to the guinea pig case. He mouthed, "She's in labor and having trouble. Tara, suit up. Wash your hands. Here's the powder, on with the gloves, girl." Tara said

The gloves had a sharp snap. She nodded.

"Pour the antiseptic over Grace's stomach," her uncle bellowed.

She did as instructed and listened as Uncle Doug whispered in the guinea pig's ear, "Gracie, you're going to be a mommy soon." The guinea pig twitched her ears and seemed to smile. Uncle Doug's lips were pinched as the ever so sharp knife edged down the swollen pig's stomach. Blood!

She dabbed his forehead with a clean white cloth.

A baby squealed. Two, three, no four little furballs, eyes red and some black in color, and they were opened. The baby guinea pigs were walking, no running around, and eating pellets. Uncle Doug continued with mommy pig. Now sewn, she was in a cage next to her babies, resting.

Glancing at the wall clock, it was a little pass noon and lunchtime. The dogs to be adopted were in their kennels, barking, and needed exercise. Uncle Doug volunteered. He gathered leashes for the ten dogs. They were different sizes and different breeds. He walked them from the shelter's back entrance to a fenced-in grassy area where they could yelp and run. The dogs had been nurtured or spayed so their personalities of different sex even out.

He pulled from his pocket a snack bar and an apple. He breathed in the fresh air and, like the dogs, enjoyed freedom. He checked the time. It was now 1:15 p.m.

A light touch feathered on his forearm. He turned his head and with a tip of his index finger scooted his Stetson back. With foot propped on the bottom fence rail and slow uplifted smile, he said, "What can I do for you, Miss Jill?"

Not removing her hand from his arm, she said, "I'm sorry. I only have your first name, but, Doug, are you available for dinner? My treat home cooking." She batted her big dewy brown eyes and waited.

"Ma'am'?"

"Tonight, I wish to thank you properly in the matter of taking such good care of my Butch. I know he's getting old, but I've had him since he was five weeks old."

Doug nodded and his uplifted smile deepened, reviling a dimple. He drawled, "And I thought you just wanted my company." He chuckled. "Last name is Symth."

Jill licked her lips and somewhat blushingly said, "I do want your company, so what do you say, cowboy?"

"Well, little lady, since Butch will be spending the night here at the clinic, how about I cook for you, say seven tonight." He pointed over his shoulder at the tiny house. "Just knock once, I'll hear ya."

She patted his arm. "I understand Butch must spend the night, and I'm glad you're close by. See you at seven tonight." She batted her bright brown eyes again.

He stood captivated and unable to move as he watched Miss Jill walk to her vehicle. He shivered, but was not cold . As he whistled for the dogs, he thought, about Jill. *She's no bigger than a minute and spunky.* He kicked the ground, "Now why did I ask her to dinner?" He settled the dogs inside the animal shelter and, after feeding and watering, searched out Tara and graveled, "Where's the nearest grocery store?"

Tara giggled. "Ms. Jill Price is quite a fireball. Here's a little insight. She has a spread not too far from here, one of the last standing. A thriving cattle farm she inherited from her grandfather several years ago, and she is known for her Spanish foals. Jill works harder than most men. You better watch out." She kept giggling. "Jill makes a mean apple pie."

"Come on, Tara, it's just dinner. You know with her being so upset about her dog." He rolled his blue eyes that matched Tara's. Then said, "Besides, I'll be moving on in three months. Yep, just *me*"—emphasizing me—"and my tiny house."

"Uncle Doug, if you say so, but I saw the way you looked at her, and I watched her body language as she interacted and gently touched you." Tara winked and said, "The nearest all-in-one store is on Route 165, 'Meyers.'" She removed her lab coat, washed her hands, and said, "It's off to school for me. Uncle Doug, enjoy your evening. Don't do anything I wouldn't do." She giggled.

He said, "I hear your cell phone ringing, so who's calling you on your private number?" His eyebrows arched.

She waved, climbing the stairs to her office, grinning, then answered, "Hello, this is Tara Scott." She held a breath and faltered. "Theodor?"

"Hello back at you. Sorry about Thursday night. Conflict in my schedule, but I have this evening available. Are you free?"

*Oh,* she thought, *am I free,* "Yes, tonight is good."

"Great. I'll pick you up at 6:30 p.m. at your house." The line went dead.

Tara looked at her phone. "It's almost 2:30 p.m." She went into her office and closed the door. Over the next two hours, she worked on line with her school studies.

The afternoon schedule was light. Doug knocked on her office door. He was whistling. "It's almost five p.m. Tara girl, clean up done and laundry is drying."

She bid her uncle good-bye and rushed from the building. She flagged the bus and arrived home at five thirty. Snow greeted her in a playful way, and the guinea pigs began squealing. She placed a finger in her ear and called her neighbor. "Hi, is Sammy home from school? I could use her help tonight."

"Wait," her mother said.

"Hi, Tara, what's ya need?" Sammy asked.

"Sammy, can you come over by six thirty tonight and do the usual, let Snow out and feed and water him then feed my critters. There's a five dollar bill in it for you."

"I'll be there and thanks."

Tara showered then pulled out blouses, slacks, dresses, and finally settled on her newly purchased tight jeans and scoop neck, red, three-quarter sleeve sweater. She selected red flats and matched with coach purse. "I'm glad for Uncle Doug. He called it a woman's gift, my purse." She added a little blush, mascara, and applied soft-red lip gloss. The doorbell dinged. She carried earrings in hand and opened the door. Glancing up, it was him smiling in that confident intriguing way. She giggled for a second time and felt warm all over. She eyed him from head to toe and back. He wore jeans that were molded to his legs, a cream-colored cranberry shirt, which stretch across his broad chest. And on his feet were an expensive pair of loafer. She thought, *He looks as good in jeans as in his tailor-made suits.*

Theodor leaned in smiling and handed her a bouquet of daisies. His woodsy aftershave wavered under her nose. She gasped and reached for the foyer table. Snow, at that very moment, chose to jump up on Theodor. His black eyes widened, and Theodor adjusted his feet then reached down and patted Snow's head. The bell dinged. The neighbor girl arrived. Tara held the daisies and said, "Thank you. Um, Theodor, sit while I put the lovely flowers in water?" Not waiting for an answer, she left the room.

# Chapter 3

THE GUINEA PIGS were impatiently squealing and kept bumping their water bottles on the side of their glass cage. Theodora let out a held breath and sat on the couch. Sammy popped her gum then took Snow by the collar. "Outside, boy." The dog followed, wagging his floppy tail. She looked over her shoulder and said, still popping her gum, "My name is Sammy, neighbor kid next door. Are you Tara's new Internet boyfriend?"

Tara froze. She took a quick glance at Theodor, and his brows were near his forehead. No answer. Tara placed her earrings in her ears and said, "I'm ready to go if you are?"

He nodded, stood, opened the front door, and followed Tara out. At the car, he opened her door and said, "You're an attractive woman."

Tara smiled and shyly said, "Not so bad yourself."

His smiled broadened, his black eyes darkened, as he slid behind the wheel of his BMW. He started the engine and backed out on to White Road. Theodor turned slightly. "I don't really suppose you're a client of mine or even a friend of a client of mine, are you?

"Do you have a need for a financial advisor?" His black eyes danced.

She bit on her lower lip and held her hands in a death grip. She whispered, "No, none of the above. However, I can explain." She shifted in her seat, her chin tilted.

He pulled into Applebee Restaurant's parking lot and opened the car door for her.

*What a gentleman*, she thought.

Chuckling, he smoothly placed a hand on her back and said, "Can't wait to hear your explanation!"

How was she to think or manage to talk with his hand's warmth piercing through her lower back? She restrained from squirming. The manager called him by name and personally seated them. He said, "Happy Birthday, Mr. Theodor Welch."

Tara batted her large blue eyes as though she were a deer caught in bright headlights. She screeched, "Birthday? How old are you, Theodor Welch?" She reached for her water glass.

His brow squinted. "Call me Theodor, and I'm a red-blooded, single thirty-seven-year-old man. So what about you?"

She licked her lips and said, "I'm not like, perhaps most women you know, who fall all over the place for you and your hot body. I'm rambling, I'm sorry."

"You think I have a hot body?" He laughed.

"Well, happy birthday, Theodor." She leaned forward. "And are we a party of two or are you expecting a group?" She looked around.

He broke out into a hardy laugh. "Only us. Are you disappointed?" He reached for her hand.

She patted his and removed her other hand.

He winked and said, "What would you like to drink?" He was surprised how relaxed he felt and enjoyed their battering and her apparent modesty.

"Sweetened iced tea."

He raised a hand to the waiter, called him over, and ordered two sweetened iced teas and a variety platter of appetizers. He tilted his head in Tara's direction. "All right, care to clarify as to why you contacted me?" The corner of his mouth lifted and a single dimple showed.

Tara silently scolded herself. She was staring at his enticing black eyes and suddenly realized he was looking intently into her blue eyes. She wondered, *Could his awesome black eyes get any darker?* Then another dimple on his right cheek appeared, and his black eyes did dance and seemly held a secretive mischief. She opened her mouth to speak and stop. Saved by the bell, their appetizers had arrived.

He handed her a small plate with the serving prongs. "Help yourself and dig in."

She placed several mild wings and bacon cheese potato skins on her plate then passed the prongs over to him. Tara bowed her head and quietly prayed. Lifting her head and with hand to mouth, she enjoyed a potato skin. She blotted her lips. "I thought you were starving."

He nodded and said, "My mother prayed at mealtime. It was years ago. She's deceased now."

"I'm sorry about your mother being gone, but prayer is good." She questioned in her thoughts, *Should I ask what happened?* Tara glanced up.

"May I call you Tara?"

She nodded.

"You remind me of her in a good way..." His voice trailed. "Happier times." He munched on the hot wings and grabbed the iced tea then reached for another hot wing. He didn't stop eating until ten ravished wing bones were in a pile. He blotted his mouth and placed six potato skins to his plate. He scarfed them down. Theodor nodded and asked, "You ready to order? I'm ravenous."

Tara laughed and asked, "What are you having?"

He laid the menu down. "Steak with fried potatoes, three eggs over easy, raisin toast, and coffee black. You?"

She thought, *Breakfast hum.* "I'll have three eggs with corn beef hash, wheat toast, and a glass of milk, white."

He chuckled, stretching out his long legs. "It's nice to see a woman who really eats. Not just ordering a salad. You're a woman after my own heart."

Tara blushed; *I would like a chance at his heart.* She replied, "I do enjoy food, always have. I work hard, study hard, and…" She didn't finish.

He finished for her, "And play hard?"

The waiter brought their food. After a few bites, she said, "I really don't have much time to play." She forked eggs into her mouth and sipped milk. "I just turned thirty, and with the responsibility and overhead of the animal shelter, plus attending online college." A bite of toast and then another. "And my veterinarian test is next week. In which I hope to obtain my veterinarian license." She ate more, drank some milk, and then continued, "My only uncle, Doug Symth, in this whole wide world on my mother's side is a veterinarian. He volunteered to help out in the clinic so it can stay open." She laid her fork down. "Doug travels now with a tiny house, so adorable, compact, comfortable, and very rustic. Inside the tiny house is a loft bedroom, surprisingly holds a king-size bed, and on the main floor an entertainment area, a kitchen, and a bathroom."

He nodded and scooped up his toast.

Tara explained, "My uncle recently retired from his career in horse training and cow punching. He's a real cowboy and is free to travel when the mood hits him. I'm blessed he's helping me out. That's another answer to prayer."

"Your uncle sound interesting. Perhaps I'll get to meet him." Theodor smiled, shifted, and said, "Tara, why not take some time to enjoy life. Everyone needs a little relaxation now and then."

Blushing from neck to face, she said, "Were you offering your services?"

He ran his index finger around the neck of his shirt and searched her face narrowing his eyes. "Tara, why did you text me?"

She bunched her full lips. "Well"—placing a napkin over her plate and not looking at him—"here's the deal. I searched dating websites seeking a male suitable to date with like faith and interest in hope of finding my soul mate. As I said before, my time is limited." She tipped her milk glass.

"May I ask what website?" His brows rose.

"'True Hearts' website, the man's post read sincere and that he was searching for true love." She stiffened. "I thought maybe so I sent the text." She glanced up at him. "However, my text miss-text and came to you instead. Now you know my explanation." She hunched her shoulders and blushed.

He nodded, crossing his arms across his chest. His muscles rippled.

Still pinkish, a tear slid down her cheek. "I'm sorry about the confusion, but when we finally met and went to the coffee shop, I wasn't aware I had typed in the wrong phone number, and that you were not him. Later I figured out my mistake. When texting in the number, the last digit was off by one." She blew her nose. "You were so kind in offering me a ride home, and it was after I went inside I thought over your conversation and realized you only talked about your company, the location, your business trips, and it hit me, you all but asked me if I needed a financial advisor." She scooted her chair and stood. "Now, Theodor, when I received your text again, I only fooled myself into believing that you had discovered my text error." She silently thought, *Perhaps someone like you could be interested in me.* "But was I ever wrong!"

He stood and walked behind her. "Please don't be upset," he breathed. "Thanks for being honest, stay a while longer, I would like for us to get better acquainted." He stepped to her side, his smile deepened, and Theodor winked. "After all, I am single and today is my birthday!"

Tara shook her head. "I've done enough damage by taking up your precious time. You're a busy man." She placed a hand in the air. "I'm going home. I've arranged for a cab." She forced a smile. "Happy birthday, Mr. Welch. Please stay and don't follow after me."

He reached for her arm. She brushed his hand away, turned, and walked out the restaurant, hailing her cab. She gave the address and sat back, thinking, *How embarrassing and what a terrible misunderstanding of who's who.* She willed back the tears.

⚜

The cabbie said, "You're here, miss. The fare is eighteen dollars."

She pulled out a twenty dollar bill she really hadn't plan on using for it was some of her grocery money and handed it to the cab driver. She sighed, "Home." Opening the door, Snow bolted to her. She petted his head and walked to the living room. Sammy was watching TV. Tara handed her the five dollar bill and said her thanks and tried to smile.

Tara flopped down and the flood gate of tears poured. She thought, *I really liked everything about him. Darn website and darn text.*

⚜

Theodor all but fell down reaching for a chair. He ran a hand over his face and muttered, "What just happened here? It's my birthday. Women don't walk out on me!" Collecting the check, he flipped out his charge card filled in the tip area and waited for his card and receipt.

The restaurant manager insisted, "Here, take your birthday cupcake with one candle home, sir."

He thought, *All I need now is a birthday horn to blow.*

⚜

He pulled out from the lot in his BMW and went straight to his gated townhouse. Inside, he flipped the dimmer light, switched on his music—opera—and cheered, "Happy Birthday to me!" He threw his keys on the coffee table. In the bedroom, he folded the cover down and left the silk sheets in place. Theodor slipped off his clothes, pulled on his stripped lounge pants, and said, "If I were a drinking man, I would pour me something strong and straight." Instead, he laid on the king-size bed with hands under his head trying to sort out his thoughts. *Nope, I hadn't a clue that Tara Scott didn't need financial service or advice.* Although, setting up and swinging his feet over the side of the bed, he said, "I am strangely attracted to her. She's petite, and those ocean-blue eyes, and soft full lips."

He paced the floor. She's not even my type of woman. She's not sophisticated, model tall, paper thin, or well-known. She's a struggling modern businesswoman who's wholesome." He found himself smiling and glanced at the clock, 3:00 a.m. "I need sleep. My day is packed with clients." He thought of Miss Tally. How was he to explain Tara Scott's text. His head hurt. "Oh, and there's the financial advisor interviews that's scheduled."

An hour later, Theodor said, "Why did Tara kiss my cheek? Was it a kiss of thank-you or just maybe she's attracted to me? Reading women is a specialty, one in which I've never had a problem with, until Tara."

He showered, shaved, and then selected a navy blue suit. Theodor reached for a lightly starched blue oxford shirt, and instantly, an image of Tara's blue eyes flashed before him. "Get a grip, Theodor." He shoved his feet into his Capture shoes and took one last look in the mirror, tousling his hair with added gel. "You've looked worst." Theodor straightened his pin-striped blue tie and left his townhouse. "Starbucks, here I come."

Starbucks was closed so he settled for White Castle coffee, open twenty-four hours a day.

Arriving at his building, Theodor opened the wide door and entered Welch Edwin Jays Investments, passing the empty seat of Miss Tally and entering into his office where different-sized balloons darted to and fro in the air. A huge sign was posted overhead marked "Happy Birthday Big 37 and Best Wishes!" He batted the balloons and sat down closing his eyes for a moment and said, "I suppose Tara Scott will move on now and connect with Internet man, Mr. Soul Mate." His stomach churned.

Rolling his shoulders, he powered up the computer and type in notes of his clientele's updates and then e-mailed investment information to them.

Miss Tally walked in and blew a horn. "Some surprise party, Mr. Welch, you were due back in the office last night," she said, pointing to his schedule.

He felt like a school boy caught. "I'm sorry, Miss Tally, for spoiling your surprise, but I was really surprised this morning when I came in to work." He stood up and swung Miss Tally around and kissed her on the forehead. "Thank you for being loyal, thoughtful, and covering for me."

She smacked his arm—tsk-tsk—and started walking out of his office, turned, and said, "First chance you get, I would like to hear about Tara Scott, however, your first person has arrived and is here early for their financial advisory interview. His name is Mr. Kevin Tillman."

Theodor got up from his chair and made quick steps behind Miss Tally, glancing in the waiting area where he saw a thin rail of a man, clean cut, not in a designer suit, but still his appearance was dressed for success. Stepping forward, Theodor called out the name, "Mr. Kevin Tillman."

The man stood, spine straight with briefcase in hand, a smile and right hand stretched out, and said, "I'm he. Call me Kevin."

Small talk was made and a few exchanges between the men; then Theodor said, "Let's move in to conference room number 2." A few minutes later, he motioned and said, "Please take a seat and do you have resume and references?"

Kevin nodded, reached into his camel-colored briefcase, and then rose, handing both resume and personal references to Theodor.

"Please sit." Theodor carefully reviewed the man's resume, looked up, and stated, "You attended Capital State then transferred to the Ohio State University, graduating this past spring 2015?" He tilted his head.

Kevin nodded and scooted to the edge of his chair. "Mr. Welch, I held a 4.0 grade. And you, sir, carry quite the reputation in financial investment and integrity obtaining clientele. I want to work for such a man and be employed here. I have worked as an understudy in the university financial department." Kevin's brown eyes widened.

Theodor penciled notes and finally said, "Mr. Tillman, Kevin, care for coffee?"

"Always, black please."

Theodor pushed the call button. "Miss Tally, we'll have that coffee now. Thank you." He glanced at the man's references. "All seemed to be in order."

After a sip, Theodor said, "A background check will be done and calls made to your references. May I have your driver's license to make a copy for our file on you?"

Kevin stood and placed his cup on the desk coaster and blew out a held breath. "Mr. Welch, I have a state ID. I'm an epileptic. Although through medication, my seizures are under control." He gazed down at the floor then stared directly into Theodor's squinted black eyes. "In my earlier days, the spells came on at variety times, they were uncontrollable. So I never acquired a driver's license. Is having a driver's license a requisite?"

Theodor pinched his nose and finished his coffee. He glanced over at Miss Tally. "Yes, Mr. Welch?" Miss Tally asked.

"Take Mr. Kevin Tillman's documents and make a copy of his state ID."

She reached for the folder and received the state ID, then looked down through her oversized white-rimmed glasses and asked, "Will that be all, sir?"

"Yes, thank you," Theodor said. "Mr. Tillman, follow Miss Tally. She will set up a callback time for you should everything check out fine." Theodor stood, shook hands with Kevin, and was pleasantly surprise that his handgrip was firm.

Morning to late afternoon, Theodor interviewed people and was out of coffee. He considered each applicant. Some were cocky and arrogant, some lacked in experience, others had too many demands, and flirts, which most certainly was not his idea of a company fit. He closed his eyes for a moment and thought, *Then there was Mr. Kevin Tillman, face before him with sincerity, and his appeared humbleness, with a touch of longing.* Theodor left his office and building to breathe in the fresh air, decided the gym was a must.

After an hour, his neck and shoulders were strained, and his legs burned from the ridged workout regimen. He changed into his swimsuit, continuing his workout in the Olympic-sized pool doing ten laps. Theodor pulled up and sat on the poolside, flipping his head and slicking back his dark hair from his eyes. He noticed women of all sizes and ages ogling him. He silently smiled and stood knowing every eye was following him as he walked toward the men's locker room to shower and dress.

In the evening, he returned to the office and checked his e-mails. *Miss Tally's e-mail concurred references from each applicant were called and she was waiting on their call back,* he thought. *Background checks had been issued.* His stomach rumbled. It was 5:30 p.m. He rose, walked from his office, locked up the building, and drove his BMW to Marcello Restaurant. His stomach sounded, he said, "Hold on, great food awaits."

Theodor finished off the garlic bread with the last bite of home-cooked Italian spaghetti. Patting his stomach, he was glad for the gym workout earlier. Checking his smartphone, he saw a message from Miss Tally: "Pack light, head to airport, you're the guest speaker tomorrow evening at seven o'clock in the Advisor's Conference room at South Beach, Florida. The initial speaker canceled, wife having triplets in crisis labor. You're scheduled there two days. All arrangements have been made. Remember we still haven't had our talk regarding Tara Scott, and I'm all ears. Send me your updated client's results and stay in touch."

He scrub over his face, paid the bill, and left Marcello Restaurant. Not having time to travel to his townhouse, he backtracked to his office. Theodor grabbed his oversized duffle bag, shaving kit, shirt, tie, and unmentionables, throwing everything in. He zipped his spare suit kept in the office in the suit bag and rushed to the airport thinking, *This is my life.*

# Chapter 4

ON BOARD THE flight, Theodor sat back to enjoy three and a half hours of quietness.

He was alerted only when the jet was to land. Out through customs and into his rental vehicle, a Seville Cadillac with sun roof, Theodor chuckled. "Oh, that Miss Tally. She thinks of everything." Fifty-three minutes later, and by setting his new watch an hour earlier, he arrived at the hotel Marriott.

He admired the suite and unpacked. Theodor pulled the covers back, shimmy from his clothes, and showered. He adjusted the overhead rain shower head and spread his arms out, letting hot water beat down across his neck and shoulders. After towel drying, he decided not to shave until morning. He lied on his side, closed his eyes, and flashed back to another time. His mother prayed on bended knee with him near as a child. He turned on his other side, and his mind returned to the restaurant the time Tara Scott prayed. He jolted wide awake and blew out a sigh.

"What's happening here? Why the comparison, mother to Tara? I must be really drained." Theodor padded to the kitchenette and reached for a bottled water and then another. He padded back to bed, lied on his back, and watched the ceiling fan go round and round. "I ate too much Italian food." He closed his eyes willing sleep. An hour later after hitting his pillow, sleep came.

He woke in sweat, running a hand through his hair. It was only a dream. Tara Scott was chatting and laughing with the man from the dating website. He felt weak and his chest ached.

"I should expect her to move on with Mr. Right, but what? Do I want to see her again?" He blinked, and her ocean-blue eyes haunted him. His body warmed.

Theodor didn't need the wakeup call. He showered again using cold water, shaved, and carefully dressed. He called the front desk and arranged for his blue suit to be sent out for cleaning.

"I'll suffer through my limited wardrobe." His hair now twisted with gel, admired in the mirror his practiced smile showing his perfectly white straight teeth. A slight dimple appeared on his right cheek, just like his father's. He squared his shoulders. He was ready to take on the world, or at least his meeting, only he had most of the day to kill.

While descending the steps, he went for a walk and saw multiple buildings emerge, a small coffee shop, ice-cream parlor, a sweetshop, and surfer sportswear and casual clothing store, he entered. Within an hour, he pulled out his charge card and purchased sandals, a polo shirt, one pair walking shorts, a bathing suit, sunscreen lotion, and beach towel. He strolled into the coffee shop and headed to the restroom, changed clothes, and ordered a black coffee; then he sat down.

The beach was within walking distance and there, Theodor found a public lounge chair and looped his towel, pulled off his polo shirt, and edged out of the sandals. Women were mostly sunbathing. He flashed them his automatic smile and ambled to the water. It was a balmy sunny day for the season, and the water was refreshing. Theodor swam to a fifty-foot Bowie and wasn't breathing hard. He swam toward the shore and tread water entertaining himself. He noticed the blotchiness of his skin. "Crap! I forgot to put on sunscreen." Swimming to shore and now with sunscreen applied, he pulled on his shirt and sat down under an umbrella for shade.

The women walked by, smiled, and flirted with him, stretching, tipping their sunhats, and batting their lashes. He closed his eyes in disgust, questioning, "Why haven't I hooked up with a pretty woman or two in the last month?" One thought, *Tara Scott*. He glanced at his watch; lunch had been missed. Another hour passed. Reaching for the beach towel, he shoved on the sandals and went back to the hotel. Theodor felt uneasy, restless even. He ordered in and flicked through the TV channels. He dosed. The doorbell dinged; his blue suit arrived. "Showtime."

It was thirty minutes until he gave his motivational speech on financial investments and their needs and usage. He checked his smartphone—a message from Miss Tally. "Tara Scott scheduled an appointment with you day after tomorrow. Time: four thirty p.m. Break a leg tonight." He adjusted his tie. His name was called. With an automatic smile in place, he said, "Hello, everyone. It's great to be here this evening in South Beach, Florida!" The seminar continued, questions were asked, and he added more clientele.

In his suite's room, he texted Miss Tally: "We need to talk. One hundred new signed clients. Have you heard back on Mr. Kevin Tillman?"

He said, "Man, I could use a drink," but instead found himself praying, "I don't remember a time I've personally sought You out. Are You even listening to me up there?" He sat down and placed his head in his hands. "What do I call You, Father, God, Jesus? I'm so confused." He got onto his knees. "I come to You about a woman named Tara Scott. I'm experiencing conflicting emotions that I've never experience before. She reminds me of my mother. I need a sign in what to do. Oh this is, Theodor Welch." He rose, showered, and let the waters cascade over him. He didn't have any instant answers, but he was breathing easier. He lied down and pulled the covers midway. Sleep came.

A knock sounded on the door. "Wakeup call, time is ten a.m."

"What? I've never slept in that late." He paused and glanced upward and breathed out, "Thanks…" He dressed in his new shorts, pulled on the polo shirt, slipped into his sandals, grabbed his swimming trunks, towel, and went downstairs hoping the breakfast bar was still open. Surprisingly, the eating area was still crowded. He began to leave when an elderly couple motioned for him from their table.

"Hi, lad, are you here for the 'Financial Enlightening Seminar'?"

He straightened and said, "You could say so, I'm the speaker," and forked his scrambled eggs.

The older man nodded and said, "We'll be there tonight, me and Annabelle. Hope to hear why I should invest at my age." They stood and hand in hand left the room.

His eggs were cold, but he still ate. He picked up a left newspaper and flipped to the investment page. He sipped his coffee. Sometime later, he slipped into his rental car, checking out the sights. He stopped at South Beach Museum and moseyed the aisles and paused at the modern art display, a face-within-a-face art piece captured his eye and wallet. A few walls over displayed the traditional art, typical basket holding fruit: apple, banana, orange. He chuckled. In another room on table display were jewelry pins connecting to the history of the Levites. On the other side of the aisle stood an aged 1800s Bible, which was protected under glass. As he circled the room, a display case was filed with artifacts, flint, arrows, and a row of nails, and a section showcasing some pure gold nails dating back to 931—970 BC to the time of King Solomon. He walked down the hall and wandered into the next room. It featured outlined dinosaurs, twenty counted in all. Down the hall, construction was underway in the south part of the building. Plastic hung from ceiling to floor and giant ropes were latched across to block off entry. He left the building.

At the beach, the water was refreshing. After two hours of swim, he sat in the lounge chair. This time with protective sunscreen lotion on. His stomach growled. Looking away up on the beach, he saw a foodie shack, the sign—flip burgers, hotdogs, French fries, onion rings. Not a healthy diet, but yummy. He rested for another half hour then headed back to the hotel. Time 4:00 p.m. He stifled a yawn and shook his head, "Shower here I come." He toweled dried and wrapped in an enormous bathrobe furnished by the hotel, set his smartphone's alarm, and flung on the bed. He blinked and yawned again. The fan blades circled round and around. Alarm sounded. Time: 5:30 p.m. Theodor stretched. "That was awesome sleep!"

An hour later, he was waiting on the sidelines in the conference room waiting to be called on the platform. The lights lowered then raised, Theodor stepped forward.

"Hello, everyone, thanks for coming, let's talk why invest, money, and more money!" He waved to the elderly couple he met earlier. And the applause began. He stressed strategies of the risk of random investing versus traditional investing. He advised the younger aged group listening that risk investments can be profitable if one rides out the long-term investment, thirty, forty, even fifty years. He explained traditional investing and in the safety of savings account, bonds, or in short-term IRAs. His time was up. Questions flowed. Fifty new clients were added to his company and twenty or so individuals reached for his business card.

Heading from the conference room, he hoped to quickly return to his suite, pack, turn in the rental vehicle, and catch a flight home. However, the elderly couple flagged him in the lobby and asked more questions. Theodor glanced at his watch, smiled, and after some time, asked, "Would you oppose to scheduling an appointment for us to discuss your options in investing?" He noticed the man's wife squeezed his hand.

"Yes, we would be agreeable. When?" the man asked.

Looking at his smartphone, Theodor said, "Would one week from tomorrow, Friday the thirteenth, work for you?"

The balding man nodded.

"Afternoon or evening? And do I need to be here in Florida or would my office do in Columbus, Ohio?"

The beefy man said, "We'll come to your office in Columbus. We are considering a move, house hunting."

Theodor whipped out his smartphone and pinned in the date and time. Name is Chestermeyer, Thomas and Annabelle. A friendly handshake completed the act, and the aging couple once again, hand in hand, walked slowly from the room.

Theodor neatly stacked the newly acquired contracts in his briefcase and darted to his suite, packed, and, at the hotel counter, checked out. The rental car was returned at the airport, and he boarded his flight on time. Thrusting through the hustle-bustle airport and people, Theodor retrieved his car and hurried to the office. He inputted the data information from South Beach clients into separate files called South Beach and keyed in their investment plans. He marked the Chestermeyer appointment on his calendar.

Miss Tally entered his office and closed the door.

Theodor motioned for her to sit down. He stood and rubbed the back of his neck. "Miss Tally, about Tara Scott, she, um, was never a client of this company or was a friend of a client." He paced, only stopping to open the aspirin bottle and pop three tables in his mouth, followed by a swallow of black coffee. Setting on the edge of his desk, he continued, "Tara's text to me was a mistake. She had searched out a dating website and found a person of interest. And thought she had texted him, finally figuring out that the text I received belonged to another man. The telephone number used was off by one digit, lucky me!"

"You remember she's scheduled in today?"

He nodded. "We've met a couple of times before I knew the whole story. When we finally met up at the restaurant, she explained, and then Tara up and walked out on me, on my birthday!" Shaking his head. "Miss Tally, Honestly, I'm confused. I cannot stop thinking of her. Sometimes her action reminds me of my mom, and Tara's so different than any woman I've ever met."

"My advice, Mr. Welch, is listen to your heart and not your head." She fluffed her handkerchief and walked toward the door, pausing. "By the way, my twin, Christy, had an emergency. She was allergic to cold medicine prescribe so I'm flying to crazy New York this afternoon to tend to her."

"But, Miss Tally…"

"Tsk-tsk, I had Mr. Tillman come in and sign most of the employment forms yesterday and gave him a crash course in phone answering. He's volunteered to fill in for me the rest of the week until further training can be provided. Mr. Welch, we need two more clerks added especially since our business growth."

"Place the ad when you come in on Monday and it's up to you to interview, hire, and train them. I trust your judgment."

A sudden knock came on doorframe. "Hello, Mr. Welch, your four thirty appointment is here. A Miss Tara Scott," Kevin said.

Miss Tally waved and wore a wide, wide smile.

Theodor blew out a breath, muttering, "She's early."

"Mr. Welch, your schedule is clear, but do you want me to meet with her? I don't mind."

"No! No, I'll be right out."

Kevin left shutting the door.

Theodor reached for the aspirin bottle again, dropping two tablets in his hand, and sat in his chair. With head in hands, he said, "Here I am again? I need Your help."

# Chapter 5

SEPTEMBER PROVED TO be a complete puzzling month; weather had been so unpredictable across the state. Harsh rain appeared at a drop of a hat, gusty winds from six to forty miles an hour without warning, and the humidity with the spike of index climbing in the mideighties. However, back at the tiny house with Doug Symth, he muttered, "I'm closing this window for a second time. The rain keeps blowing in." He stirred the spaghetti sauce that was simmering and glanced at the pan of water, waiting for it to boil to drop in the pasta. He added a sprinkle of salt. The slices of buttered garlic bread set on the counter waiting to be warm.

Doug jerked when a bombing knock sounded on the front door. He glanced out the window and saw it was Miss Jill Price. She was holding a pie. He smiled then murmured, "It's probably apple." Opening the door, he moved aside and said, "Right on time. Step in and take a load off your feet." He pointed to the living room chair. Coffee, iced tea, or?"

"Water is fine. Apron's cute." She muffled a laugh.

Glancing down and stretching out his arms, he said, chuckling, "I wouldn't be without it." He retrieved bottle water and handed it to Miss Price. He stirred the sauce then dropped the pasta in the boiling water and placed the garlic bread in the oven. "It won't be long now."

"Doug, I like your tiny house. It's comfy."

"Thanks. I had it designed to suit me."

She nodded then asked, "Did you check on Butch since you left the clinic?"

"Yes." He shut the fire off from under the sauce and the pasta. He carefully lifted the pan and drained off the liquid and piled her and his plate high. He reached the oven, turned off the switch, and placed the buttered garlic bread on a plate. "Butch is resting well. Tomorrow, he'll be more like his old self. I'm glad it wasn't worst."

Jill bowed her head and peeked up at Doug. He hunched his shoulders, and she folded her hands and prayed. They ate in comfort and quietness. She patted his arm and said, "Thank you for the invite and for cooking such a lovely dinner. The salad was fresh and crispy."

"Well, can't take no credit for that. Tara has a small garden planted, and I got the fixings out there." He turned to the pie.

"Here, let me cut the pie. You get the dishes and forks." Raising her brown eyes, she said, "Clean plates please."

Doug saluted and in seven steps had plates and forks in hand. He smacked his lips and twisted his mustache. "Miss—I mean, Jill, your pie is mouthwateringly delicious!"

She fanned herself and began clearing the dishes.

Doug, towering over her shoulder, said, "I'll wash." He shifted to her right. Their arms touch. "I think we need the window open. The air is a mighty tight in here."

She naturally picked up a dry towel and began wiping the dishes and stacking them in place. She then covered the leftover apple pie and handed it to him to make room in his tiny refrigerator. Jill glanced up. "Maybe you'll enjoy a piece of pie or two later with ice cream."

Doug shifted, filling the smallness of his one-hundred-forty-four-foot tiny house. "Care to take a peek at Butch? Of course, observing through the clinic's one-way window."

"All right, cowboy, lead the way."

His lips slowly uplifted, and he offered her his arm.

"My, my, look at the time." Jill paused at her Ford Ranger truck. "Thanks again for the meal and the evening." As she slid onto the seat, her cell phone rang. She waved out the window and reached for her phone. "Hello."

Doug inside his tiny house sat on the sofa with head in hands. "Now how did I get roped into transporting Butch to Jill's farm tomorrow night?" He stood looking out. "She hoodwinked me into a fried chicken dinner. She's something else!" He shook his head.

The next morning while working at the shelter, Doug noticed his niece seemed preoccupied and appeared unusually quiet. He supposed she was deep in thought from all the studying and with the upcoming state board veterinarian test. She stayed in her office. The day was now evening and late; he knocked on her office door. "Tara?" He knocked again. No answer. Doug turned the knob slightly, and the door opened and stood ajar. Tara was nestled on the futon with eyes closed and the reading book was on the floor still open. He quietly walked to her and placed a throw rug from the back of the futon across her. Tara squirmed then settled in. He switched the lights off and left.

Pulling his truck into the clinic's loading zone, he fetched Butch. Glancing toward Tara's office, he muttered, "She works too hard, too many hours, and adds too much pressure on herself. If it weren't for me, she'd be all alone in this world."

Butch barked and licked his face.

He situated Butch in the front seat of his black 150 Ford truck and locked the shelter's doors. He shifted into gear and headed toward Jill's farm. Ten miles later, he navigated down Borrow Road. He squinted as a light drizzle began. Doug repeated Jill's directions, "Farm third on the left." Ten minutes later, he spotted a posted sign marked Price Farm. He glanced over at the dog and said, "You're almost home, ole boy," and scratched Butch's head.

On both sides of the graveled lane, he saw cattle as far as his eye could see until only black dots appeared. Closer in were several good-sized rustic barns and a fenced-in area holding horses. He noted several bungalows were nearby. He made a slight turn, and his mouth gaped as he took in a breathtaking farmhouse. He tipped his hat. "Wow, I've worked on some large spreads in my day for wealthy owners, but this place in Grove City within a few miles of the hustle-bustle life, well, this farmhouse is amazing. Her grandfather must have had some vision. Wonder how many acres?"

He pulled the truck in front of the hitching post and turned off the engine. Sitting with hands on the steering wheel, he stared at the two-story cedar house. It was framed with a double wide mission style with wood-metal trim doors, which sprung open on a white wraparound porch. Adirondack chairs were lined in different sections. His mind transported to the homes built in Atlanta in the early 1800s.

Jill appeared and held out her arms. He blew out a held breath then remembered her dog, Butch. He climbed from the truck and said, "Butch is almost good as new. In just a few more days, he can be out and about the farm." Handing over the leash, he said, "Jill, what a beautiful spread."

She hooked arms with him. "Thanks, Cowboy, come on in. Dinner is waiting."

He shucked from his boots and in stocking feet let her lead the way. "Smells mouthwatering good."

She smiled and her brown eyes held a sparkle. She settled the dog off from the kitchen returning her attention back on Doug. The kitchen was modern, and he sat across from her, placing his hat on a chair. He flipped his napkin and placed it at his neck. She laid hers across her lap. Jill passed the fried golden-brown chicken, pausing only to take a piece. She said, "Help yourself. Go on, take another piece." The mash potatoes were passed, and she spooned on the gravy.

He took a bite of crunchy yummy chicken, eyes widened. She had bowed her head and began praying. He stopped chewing and quickly tilted his head.

She smiled and forked a bite of food. "So tell me about yourself."

Doug, for some reason, relaxed around Jill. He nodded and an uplifted smile continued to his ocean-blue eyes. He crossed his feet at the ankles. "Well, back in the day, my father expected me to follow in his footsteps, banking." Doug rolled his eyes, taking another bite of chicken. "This sure is good. I bet you could win a blue ribbon at the fair."

She smiled. "Not bragging, but I have won lots of blue ribbons. The chicken recipe was my grandmother's. She folded her hands in her lap. "So what career path did you decide?"

He chuckled. "Not banking." Twisting his mustache, he said, "I left home at eighteen and never looked back. I followed my heart in bronco riding. And I was good, better than good. After three years, I had made a name for myself on the circuit and won several first and second place awards. I used most of my winning just getting from one place to another and on other things." He winked. "From time to time, I sent newspaper clippings to my folks, only Mom wrote me a few times. On the circuit, it was hard for mail to catch up to you."

That year in the fall, the big purse for bronco riding was being held in Mexico, and I needed some extra cash to pay my entryway. So I enter a two-bit riding bull contest along the way, and I pulled the meanest bull possible called Jude Devil, which lived up to his name."

Jill covered her mouth.

"No, before you ask, he didn't throw me well, not at first, but on the way out from the shoot, that means, um, bull pushed me into the medal stockade fence. My left leg caught and was squeezed. I couldn't jerk it free. Leaving me off-balance, suddenly the bull broke loose, and I was then flipped and took a gore to the hip before being rescued."

"Oh my, dear lord."

"Three months later, I woke up in the hospital and found I had extensive surgery to the left leg. And news that I would most likely never ride professionally again." He nodded his head.

"Let me get you a piece of Apple pie and how about black coffee?" Without waiting, she stood and served him.

After a few bites, he cleared his throat and reached for his hat. "Jill, it's late. Thanks for dinner." He patted his stomach. "I have an early day tomorrow. I hope Butch stays out of trouble and leave those squirrels alone." He walked to the front door and put his feet into his boots.

She opened the door and stood on the porch. "Thanks, cowboy, for caring for Butch." She touched his jaw. "You're so thoughtful." She blinked. "If you're out this way, stop in. Door's always open. I'll show you around." On tiptoe, she kissed his cheek.

In the truck, he waved and rushed down the road as quick as he was allowed to drive. He thought, *I've never told a woman about my life, and she's a lady. Her light kiss made a zinging impact. Seeing her through the truck's mirror and waving made me almost stop the truck, jump down, grab her close, and kiss her. What was that?*

Back at the shelter, he let himself in and checked on the few held-over animals then headed to Tara's office. She was gone. He locked up and went inside his tiny house, and the rains came. "It's a good night to sleep." Doug lay listening to the pit-a-patter hitting the tin roof and slept. Awareness of Miss Jill Price entered his mind. Her thin-lip smile reached her brown eyes and warmed his insides like drinking rich hot chocolate. Her touch was soft yet connections were powerful. Her shiny black hair and her rounded full figure made him weak in the knees.

He woke startled. "I need a woman, a card game, a night out to howl."

Early the next evening, Tara entered the clinic. "Uncle Doug, Will you set aside time tomorrow and help me with the questions and the answers needed for the state board test coming up? I have test examples."

"When's the big day? And yes, tomorrow afternoon is fine. Tara, you're going to do just fine." He scrubbed his face. "Now, missy, turn around. Where might you be going dress to the hilt?"

She adjusted her slingback shoe. "I'm attending a fund-raiser with Mr. Welch. Do you think I, I…"

"My sweet Tara, that red dress will blow his socks off."

A horn honked. Doug placed a hand on her arm. "Let him come in for you!"

She waited. "How was Miss Price's fried chicken?"

He picked up the broom. "Best ever including mine. She's won all kinds of blue ribbons."

"Hello, Tara," a familiar baritone voice said.

Doug stepped in front of Tara and placed his hand outward. "I'm Tara's uncle Doug, and you are?"

Eyes said interested, but mouth said, "Friend, my name is Mr. Theodor Welch. Please to meet you. Tara has mentioned you."

His hand met Doug's pressure, and Doug said, "Likewise. Have fun. Be careful. And watch out for her." Eyes were narrowed as the two left.

Doug finished the clinic's chores and headed to his tiny house. He heated the leftover chicken Jill insisted he bring home and cut him a slice of apple pie. He poured black coffee and switched on the television. He flipped through the stations. Finding nothing of interest, he turned it off. He reached for a book—*Moby Dick*, a favorite, and settled in. After reading chapter 2 over three times, he slammed the book shut and paced.

"Why am I restless?" He walked over to the fenced yard, propped his foot on the rail, and closed his eyes and breathed in the fresh air. His cell phone rang. "Hello, Doug here."

"This is Jill. I understand you've retired from cow punching and the laborious horse days, but according to the Internet, you are the one I need to reckon with." She waited with no response.

"Doug, I need your help!" She listened. No response. "I've acquired an Arabian pedigree stallion from the Egyptian line, a purebred. I've had my eye on his lineage for a long time. However, the seven-year-old stallion has never been ridden. I'll pay good wages. Please say yes to your training."

He stuttered, "Well, Jill, thanks for the flattery, but I'm only in town for a short stay. I'm filling in, as you know, for my niece at the shelter's clinic just until she has her veterinarian license. My three-month agreement is close to an end."

"Oh, I'm sure we can work out a schedule between us. The Arabian should be settled in his new stable environment by the end of the week. I need you to check him out. Can you start Tuesday?"

He ran a hand through his brown hair. "I'll stop over and take a look at the Arabian horse. Mind you, I'm not making any promises."

"Thank you, Doug, plan on dinner. I've got to go. Bye." Line went dead.

He glared at his cell phone. Rain came; he was forced inside. Another sleepless night. *What was it about that woman?* He sat up in bed and moaned. "I've known lots of women, but they were only out for a good time, or my money and a moment of fame. I'm doing just fine without any commitments." He swung from the loft, dressed, and headed into the clinic where he powered up the computer and entered the animals' welfare data updates. He finished out the rest of the week with the successfully held adoption animal party and gave instructions of care with each placement. Seven dogs and three feline cats along with nine guinea pigs plus mom pig and siblings had been adopted by families. Doug handled all weekend emergencies and ordered supplies in the clinic for his niece. He sighed. "Leaving her would be hard, knowing Tara would be all alone." He made a silent oath promising to stay in touch. He called out, "Tara, I'm headed over to Jill's. She's asked me to take a look at her new Arabian horse."

Tara's blue eyes widened.

He backed his truck from the shelter's clinic parking lot and was whistling. He glanced in the mirror and said, "I'm only making a courteous call to Jill. After all, she's fed me with her award-winning blue ribbon fried chicken."

Jill stood on the porch, smiling. He swung from the truck, and she rushed to his side, grabbing his arm and talking nonstop until they entered the horse barn. Before them stood the most majestic, refined, stamina Egyptian-Arabian horse named Satish Adhem.

Doug's mouth gaped. "What a great beauty." He rocked on his boots. "Jill, are you planning on riding him?"

"It's definitely in my plans, but my main purpose in the purchase of the Egyptian Arabian is to breed him with my Spanish mares. With Satish Adhem's stellar pedigree and my known mares', their folds will be in high demand. What's your thoughts?"

He walked around the horse, whispered in his ear, patted him, and made eye contact. He checked out his head while touching his ears, measuring the width between the stallion's eyes. He opened the horse's lips, checking teeth /gums, then fingering down the legs and checking hoofs. He gave a cautious examination knowing not to take his eyes off the stallion. He learned a long time ago their craftiness of biting, headbutts, and kicks even when they nuzzled. Lifting his hat, he said, "He's of great strength, power, intelligence, and very praiseworthy!"

Jill took his hand and walked to the next barn, showing him the fillies of choice to breed. Again she said, "Doug, I need your help."

His heart raced.

Those bunched lips said, "The fall season is upon me and these mares need to produce their folds before the end of next year. I'm already late in planning the season." She turned, walking away. "Come on, cowboy, let's eat then we'll talk more over dessert."

The way she looked at him and said cowboy made his chest swell. He thought, *Dinner is good, then I'll bow out and leave.* He seated Jill and sat down across from her. Taking a drink of iced tea, he watched as she bowed her head, and this time, he was ready and did the same. Time passed. Doug looked at his plate; it was fit for a king, homemade pot roast. *Jill drives a hard bargain.* He glanced her way.

"Doug, dinner is included in the benefit package I'm offering you. She hit the table with fisted hand. "Now let's get your wages out of the way. Name your amount!"

He squirmed and blew out a held breath. He squared his shoulders, looked Jill in her soft brown eyes, and gave her a ridiculously high fee amount."

"Done. See you in the morning, say 6:00 a.m."

Wide-eyed Doug downed his coffee and bid her a farewell then pulled his hat down and in the truck shook his head. "Now how did she manage that?" He chuckled.

# Chapter 6

Tara Scott paced back and forth in her kitchen with Snow following her step by step, muttering to no one, "Was I ever rude to Theodor? He's been nothing but polite, and he even asked me to stay at the restaurant so we could talk. But no! What did I do? Acted like some hormonal teenager, blew up, and fled. He makes me off-balance and flustered." She flopped down. "What must he think when I adamantly told him not to follow me." She petted Snow's head.

He waggled his head and woof.

She rose and let him out in the backyard, still babbling, "Theodor is too handsome for his own good." She shivered. "Just the way he carries himself spine so straight and that smug look, he is so self-assured." She sighed. "Oh, those kind coal-black eyes that seems to see clear through me." She picked up her cell phone. "No, I'll not text him. I'll call the main office and ask for a meeting." Her heart fluttered. She closed her eyes and could see his attractive face and imagine smelling his woodsy cologne mingled with man. She sighed again. "Oh, you're a romantic Tara Scott to your own fault."

Several days passed. The state's veterinarian test was held on Thursday. The questions and her answering were long and hard. She felt rather confident for she had prepared, crammed, and studied with Doug. Now it was waiting on the test results, hoping by next Tuesday she would receive a positive phone call. She hadn't eaten or slept in a regular pattern.

Day in, day out, her uncle worked by her side and was quite the encourager. She had pushed herself to exhaustion and was noticeably a little off-balance. Midmorning Monday, he said, "You're taking the rest of the week off. Go, get relax, have fun. Don't even think of work or your test results." His smile softened. "I'll be staying around for a little bit longer." He tipped his hat. "I've agreed to help Miss Price with her newly purchased Arabian horse."

"Uncle, will you be pushing your physical self to much?"

Shaking his head, he said, "No. Baby steps. I'll begin with a lead, touch feely sort of thing, on his ears and body. When the time is right, I'll place on the halter. It takes a long while just doing the groundwork. Later, I'll attempt more by adding halter, the blanket, and saddle to his back. That's where the real work begins. Besides, the arena has plenty of room inside, and on good days eventually, we'll go outside. Don't get all worry"—he touched her cheek—"I know what I'm doing." He chuckled. "Not my first rodeo." He pointed at her cell phone.

"All right, I'm turning it off. I'm officially on sabbatical." She kissed his cheek. "Thanks."

"Where can you be reached if need be?"

"At the house or fishing in the creek. I'll be close by."

He nodded then leashed the enclosed dogs and walked them to the fenced area and let them run and yelp.

By Friday morning, Tara had stacks of clothes on her bed. It looked like a rummage sale. Tara finally chose a green pin-striped sundress with flowers embroidered around the hem. "I'm not trying to impress Theodor." Glancing in the mirror at her reflection, she said, "Yes you are." She added a little black mascara and bright-pink lip gloss matching her painted nails. She slipped on green wedge sandals then brought Snow in and said, "Guard the house," knowing he would curl up on a rug and sleep.

She arrived fifteen minutes early at the Edwin Jays Investments building and was surprised when Miss Tally handed her a mocha latte coffee. She thought, *Had Theodor mentioned me to Miss Tally.* Tara sipped and watched cautiously Miss Tally's oversized white-rimmed glasses tilter at the tip of her nose. She grinned then bent and said, "Be kind to Theodor." Miss Tally gathered her purse and whispered something in the ear of the slim man at the copier. He turned and tilted his head. Miss Tally left the office.

Tara's name was called. The time had passed quickly. Mr. Theodor Welch stood in his office doorway and was breathtaking. He stepped aside allowing her to pass and come in his office. He motioned her to sit in the high-back chair. His black eyes gave nothing away. Tara followed his height and searched his face.

Staring back, he asked, "What brings you in today?" The office phone rang. He threw up a hand, mouthing, "Sorry." Finally on the third ring, he answered, "Edwin Jay's Investments. This is Theodor Welch."

She saw his black eyes darken then blink. He stared at her, yet answered, "Of course I'll be there. Yes, two," and hung up the receiver.

"Tara"—the corner of his mouth uplifted—"I have a situation and I know it's short notice. I need your help."

She rose. "Shall I call back and reschedule?"

He came around the desk and sat across from her. "I'm scheduled to attend a formal fund-raiser tonight, and I do apologize our meeting now must be cut short." He touched her shoulder. "Tara, I'm asking, would you attend the fund-raiser with me tonight. I'll pick you up say 6:00 p.m."

She backed from the door with opened mouth and saw the rail of a man. She handed him her coffee cup and just nodded at Theodor.

In her car, Tara shivered but wasn't cold. She hadn't expected Theodor to ask for a date or whatever it was. Had he, on the spare of the moment, just needed a plus one for the evening? "I'm so pathetic. I didn't even hesitate." Driving home, she thought, *What to wear!* Tara soaked in scented bubble bath from neck down. After an hour, she towel dried and put lotion on her body with jasmine oil. She searched her closet and settled on a red dress she bought on a whim while shopping with the shelter's receptionist. She hunched her shoulders and said, "I never thought red anything went with my bright-red hair." But looking in the mirror, she had to admit red was more than kind to her. The receptionist was right; the dress hugged all her curves. She glossed her lips one more time and bent down to adjust her black sling heels. Tara fanned herself counting to ten, left her house, and drove to the clinic in her uncle's truck. She wanted his opinion on how she looked. She texted Theodor where to pick her up.

He let out a wolf whistle and said, "Girl, where are you going in that and with whom?"

"Hello, Tara!" Theodor's black eyes carried a smile.

Tara's uncle met him with a friendly handshake and glared a warning.

"Call me, Tara, if you need anything." He was still eyeing Theodor.

She felt her face; it was hot. "I will." On tiptoe, she kissed Doug's cheek and whispered, "You, my uncle, better watch out for Miss Jill Price."

He leaned back on his boots laughing and shook his head.

Theodor was silent on the way to the fund-raiser. After parking, he placed a hand on her back and entered the fund-raiser room.

Theodor stayed a perfect gentleman throughout the evening and introduced Tara as his special friend. Now what did *special friend* mean? They danced, and she was on cloud nine. Other beautiful women tapped him on the shoulder yet he denied them a dance, saying, "Tara reserved her dance card for just me tonight." Then he hunched his shoulders and wore that dynamic smile.

Theodor went to the buffet bar for drinks when a striking brunette butted up to him and linked arms. His smile was intact, but his black eyes narrowed. As he moved from sight, his name was called to come on stage. Tara waited. His name was called again. Taking two steps at a time, paused, and joked. Tara thought, *His body language seems off.*

He glanced her way; she wondered, *Is he sorry in asking me to the fund-raiser?* Her shoulder was bumped. Glancing, she saw it was the stylish brunette who moments earlier stood with Theodor. The woman batted her fake lashes, which framed her cold indifferent brown eyes. The woman said, "My name is Jeanette Wyncote, and you, Miss Tara Scott, are way out of your league." She laughed huskily. "Dear, Ted and I go way back." She perched her painted red lips, adjusted her shoulders, turned, and swerved through the crowd without so much as a look back. Tara thought, *Jeanette is tall, slender, model like, and very leggy. Her raven hair styled in a sophisticated upsweep, and her perfect makeup smooth as glass on her porcelain skin. She smelled very perfumery.*

Tara coughed and fleetingly looked toward the stage and captured another vision of Theodor. However, that woman was on stage giving him a kiss and not on the cheek! Tara felt angry. Holding back tears, she rushed to the door and glanced again toward Theodor. He was holding the painted-up woman's hand. A tear dropped. It was definitely time to leave. She reached into her clutch purse and hit speed dial.

"Uncle Doug."

"Tara, you all right?"

Sniffling, she said, "Come pick me up! I'm in the lobby of the Southern Hotel. It's on South High Street. Hurry." Her voice cracked.

"You all right?" There was only silence.

Tara caught Doug's eye. He wrapped his arms around her and muttered something she couldn't understand. She cried. He helped her walk to his truck, opened the door, and lifted her up, placing the seatbelt in lock position. He peeked at the hotel doors.

She was glad there was no Mr. Welch.

In the truck, Doug turned the music on low. "Want to talk?"

She sobbed. "No." And hiccupped.

He drove in quietness. Reaching her house, he opened the door and carried her in.

He sat Tara at the kitchen table and made her Chamomile tea. "Here, drink this." Uncle Doug, in quietness, ran hot bathwater and added Found & Flora bubble oil. He leaned against the kitchen counter and stared at her. "What happened? What did he say or do?"

"Nothing. Not a thing, that's the problem." Tara locked eyes with her uncle's, and the tears began again.

"Tara, soak in the tub. I read somewhere it helps. Your old nightshirt and robe is on the hook in the bathroom. I'll take care of Snow. Go." He reached into his back pocket and handed her his handkerchief.

She obeyed. Tara didn't know how long she soaked but woke to a dim light filtering under the bathroom door. She padded into the kitchen and turned on the water then reached for a glass. Tara padded back to her room and went to bed. She pulled the covers over her head, fading in and out of sleep. She glanced at the table clock, two thirty. She sighed. In a wary, tossing and turning, the hurting words came: *You're out of your league.* She wondered, *Why*

*did Theodor asked her to the event in the first place since porcelain doll*
*would be at the fund-raiser?*

A pounding noise wrapped on her front door. Snow barked. The pounding sound came again this time; it was louder. Snow kept barking. Tara slipped into her trusty old robe and slid into her pink fluffy slippers and walked into the living room. She heard two men's voices, mostly Uncle Doug's shouting. She walked toward the voices. Rubbing her eyes in disbelief with mouth opened, she could do nothing. Tara stopped and stared. Uncle Doug threw a punch, and Theodor took a right hook to the jaw landing him on the floor.

The familiar baritone voice said, "What was that for? I told you I don't know why she decided to leave me at the fund-raiser event." Rubbing his jaw, Theodor stood. "That's why I'm here so we can talk."

Doug raised his fist. "You better never bother Tara again. She deserves more! Get out." The front door was still open. Doug motioned Theodor to leave, still shouting, "Now! There's more where that came from." He raised his fist. The door slammed.

Uncle Doug turned and walked over to Tara. "I know it wasn't the Christian thing to do, but it felt good." Grinning, he said, "Righteous wrath is everything.

"Maybe I should call him."

"No." He placed an arm around her waist and herded her back into bed. "Get some sleep." He kissed her forehead.

The sun was dancing with shadows in her bedroom. Tara hadn't slept but didn't want to get dress either. It was past time to be at the clinic; however, when she entered, Doug shooed her out of the shelter's doorway. "I thought you might try to come into work. It's not happening. Jill called and you're due out at her place. I made arrangements for you to go horseback riding." He used shooing motions. "Be sure and see Satish Adhem, remember? The Arabian horse. Did you know Jill has several riding trails on her spread?"

Tara shook her head.

"Take my truck. Keys are in it. I'll call you when I lock up."

Tara had questions but didn't ask. She hopped in the truck and drove to Jill's. Jill was waiting with two saddled horses. Tara followed without a word. After several hours, Jill stopped her horse and said, "Let's take a break."

Being October, surprisingly, the sun was bright and warm, almost hot. They sat in the shade, and Tara enjoyed the lunch Jill provided. Jill said, "Tara, tell me about him?"

"Who, Uncle Doug?"

"No! The man who has you tied up in knots. I see it in the way you act."

Tara blew out a held breath. "Jill..." The tears dropped uncontrollably. "I'm sorry."

Jill took her hand and gave it a squeeze. "Talking helps. Take your time."

"Well, where to begin?" She let out a breath. "I texted a man I thought was with the dating website I searched and discovered later Theodor wasn't that man. I don't know how it happened, but I've formed feelings for Theodor. You know Mr. Welch is wealthy, and single, owner of a building and manages his own investment company. Women fall at his feet. In the beginning when he received my text, he assumed I was a past client or a friend of a client."

Jill patted her hands. "Now, now, things have a way of working themselves out. When Mr. Welch figured out you weren't his client or a friend of a client, what happened?"

Tara looked across the land. "After I explained my mix-up in texting him, I was embarrassed. We were at a restaurant, our meal almost over. Theodor still asked me to stay at the restaurant to get better acquainted, but I left. Then I felt ashamed of myself for being rude. After several weeks, I called his office and made an appointment. I only wanted to apologize to Theodor. However, he received a phone call immediately upon my being seated in his office. I waited. He hung up the receiver and said, 'I need your help, will you attend the investor's fund-raiser with me tonight?'"

"So he asked you out on a date?"

"I don't know, really. He did pick me up at 6:00 p.m. to attend the fund-raiser event. And he stayed by my side, danced only with me. He was wonderful. But everything went downhill when he went after drinks. It sounds silly now." Tara rolled her eyes. "While he was waiting at the bar, a gorgeous model-looking woman approached him. I stood on my tiptoes and saw she placed a hand on his arm and watch them disappear. The announcer on stage called his name for a second time." Tara turned and searched Jill's face.

"Well, what happened?"

"I didn't get a drink and then that woman who disappeared with Theodor bumped my arm and huskily said, 'Ted and I have been friends for a long time.' She slithered away ending on stage with him where they kissed."

"Whoa wait! He kissed her?"

"No, not exactly. She kissed him. He held her hand. I left."

Jill folded the tablecloth and placed leftovers in her saddlebag. "So is that how your uncle hurt his hand? Defending you?"

"What? Did he say he hit Mr. Welch?" She looked pale.

With hand on hip, she replied, "Yep, but not why."

"It's a hot mess, Jill. Uncle Doug ordered him never to contact me again, and he ordered me to take the week off. Today, he shushed me from the shelter."

"Saddle up, girl." No more was said.

Tears had stopped and their ride back was quiet. At the barn, Tara brushed down her horse and saw the magnificent Arabian. She remarked on his rich black coloring and his stature. "What a fine-looking animal, Jill."

"Stay for dinner?"

"I'll call my uncle."

"Tell him to get over here. I'm serving his favorite, meatloaf." Jill smiled.

Tara made the call and left Jill's place momentarily to pick up her uncle. At the shelter, she excused herself and went to her office. Tara applied a base powder to her face, pinched her cheeks, and added lip gloss. Her uncle was behind the wheel singing a country western song off-key, and he had defiantly put on the aftershave.

Doug parked the truck and stared ahead. Tara saw he was grinning from ear to ear; Jill was on the front porch waving. He jumped to the ground, and Jill was at his side.

"Good evening, Jill. Thanks for our dinner invite." He pulled out his hand from behind him, presenting her with a picked bouquet of flowers.

"Doug." She fanned herself. "Thank you. I've never seen prettier." Jill looped arm with him.

"Come on, cowboy, Tara, let's eat."

Doug seated Jill then Tara. He spread out his muscular arms and reached for their hands and prayed, "Thank You, Almighty for the two women in my life and for this fine meal."

As Jill raised her head, he flipped his napkin and winked. Tara stared at him and then glanced at Jill. Both were smiling like a Cheshire cat. They ate family style, and Tara took a second helping and still made room for cherry pie, her favorite.

She said, "Jill, I need to take a little walk, mine?"

"No, no, dear. We'll stroll with you. It's dark out there."

Doug lifted his dishes to the sink and started the soaking water. Jill touched his arm and led him outside. They talked about plans with him working with Satish Adhem the Arabian.

"Tara, heard anything from your state board veterinarian test?"

"Not yet, hopefully tomorrow."

Doug said, "Tara, it's time to head up the road, early morning." He helped her into the truck and walked Jill back to the front door. He leaned in and brushed her lips.

"Thanks for another wonderful meal." He lingered, touching her blushed cheek.

"Cowboy, thanks for praying."

He turned and slid under the wheel of his truck. "Well, Tara, do you feel any better?"

She nodded, wearing a silly grin until thoughts of Theodor crossed her mind; her stomach churned.

# Chapter 7

THEODOR CONSIDERED MISS Tally's words: *Why did Tara scheduled an appointment? Did she need financial advice? Or had she thought your invitation to the fund-raiser event was a date? Could Tara have feelings for you?* He touched his jaw remembering her uncle Doug's terms, *Don't ever contact her again. She deserves better.* Theodor pushed in Kevin's extinction. "Step into my office."

"Yes, Mr. Welch?"

"Call me Theodor. Are you ready to apply yourself as a financial advisor?"

"Yes, sir."

"Then make yourself available for all clients including mine until further notice. I have personal business that needs attention."

A wide grin spread across Kevin's face. "Thanks for the opportunity. I'm free to handle your schedule." Kevin headed toward the door and paused. "Although what about Miss Tara Scott?"

Theodor's eyebrows rose. "Did she reschedule?"

"She's in the lobby. I can—"

Theodor stood. "No, no, I'll take it from here. But, Kevin, you take the calls and pencil my clients into your schedule on your calendar. I'll be in touch, better yet e-mail me, text, or call me if you have any questions. However, Miss Tally is a very resourceful person. She's been known to run the office without me." He stood and stormed from his office, passing Kevin, where he approached Tara. "Hello, Miss Scott. Glad you could reschedule."

Miss Tally, not looking away from the computer, made her favorite sound. *Tsk–tsk.*

Theodor narrowed his dark eyes. "I'm on my way to a late luncheon. Will you do me the honor and join me?"

Miss Tally's eyes were like a clock's pendulum, moving back and forth on Tara and then Theodor.

"Well…" Tara bit her lower lip. "I don't."

He helped her from her seat and held her purse. "I promise to be a perfect gentleman. Scout's honor."

Miss Tally said, "Mr. Welch, you were never in the Boy Scouts." She kept keying on the computer. *Tap, tap, tap.*

Tara giggled.

"Miss Tally, I trust your sister is fine!"

He took Tara by the elbow and guided her out of the office foyer and then his building. He glanced her way. "My, you look stunning."

"Likewise. Where are we having lunch?"

"Do you like Chinese food?"

She nodded.

"'Hoy Toy' is around the corner and a favorite of mine. My mother brought me there as a boy, the best of memories."

She smiled and uncurled her fist.

They enter the restaurant and were seated in a cozy corner. The decorations were defiantly Asian. The seating area was designed with red, orange, and a bright green. She glanced around and noticed the place was almost empty.

He ordered a pot of green tea and asked, "What would you like to order in food? I'm having the house specialty with white rice."

"I would like the Wor Sue Guy with fried rice. I can almost taste it."

She unfolded her napkin on her lap and sipped the tea. Tara straightened in her seat. "Theodor."

He waited while watching her mouth move.

The waitress brought their food. He used chopsticks.

She bowed her head; he lightly touched her folded hands while she continued to pray softly. He said, "Amen." After several bites, he said, "So, Tara, what were you saying earlier? I'm afraid your beauty has distracted me, I didn't hear a thing. I'm sorry."

Her neck to face reddened.

He sipped tea and poured more.

She cleared her throat. "I would like to know why you asked me to attend the fund-raiser event with you? I must say I'm confused."

He reached for her hand and entwined her fingers with his. "Promise me first you won't bolt on me."

She blushed more.

"Tara," he began, "let me"—he locked eyes—"say I'm interested in you. I would like to pursue a real date with you." He scrubbed his face. "But to be honest, when I asked you to attend the fund-raiser with me, it was with the intentions that we could talk later on why you came to my office." His brows bunched. "I didn't think how you might take my invitation. I do, however, now realize you didn't schedule your appointment to become a new client." He saw Tara's blue eyes darken. "Now wait, please."

Tara placed the napkin over her plate. "That's correct. I didn't schedule an appointment to discuss investments. Rather, I came in to apologize for the manner in which I left the restaurant after you so kindly invited me to stay." She stood. "I like you, Theodor. I like you a lot, but we're not after the same things in life. I want the whole package with a man, love, marriage, and family." She hunched her shoulders. "Not a fling or a one-night stand, not even a passing fancy." She smoothed her dress then icily said, "Call Jeanette or one of your other accomplishments, just not me. Take me to my car!"

He nodded, paid the bill, and slowly walked with her to her car. "May I call you sometime?"

She kissed his check. "Thanks for lunch today, Theodor, and for explaining the fund-raiser circumstances, but no, please don't call me. I need to move forward, just not with you."

"Wait." He watched as she drove away.

Miss Tally was still in the office when Theodor rushed by her. She followed on his heels into his office, looking over her oversized white-rimmed glasses, which were on her nose by a thread. "Tsk-tsk, Mr. Bachelor, whose fence this time did you get caught moseying over?"

"Miss Tally."

"Don't Miss Tally me." She stomped her foot. "I've bailed you out of more women situations and scrapes than ten men. So how did you get that shiner?" She giggled.

He cleared his throat. "We need to work!"

She sat down across from him, staring. "I'm waiting."

"You came back a day early."

"I did, and my sister is on another ski trip. Thanks for asking. Now spill the beans."

The phone rang. Theodor reached for the receiver, but Miss Tally shook her head.

"Let it ring. Our new financial advisor will pick up." She stood. "Need coffee." Not waiting, she plopped a pod in the coffeemaker and then handed him a mug of steamy brew. "So how did your meeting go with Tara Scott?"

"It was interrupted. I answered the phone, and the fund-raiser committee's foreman called verifying my attendance and with a plus one invite. I invited Tara to attend with me since she was in the office instead of calling…well, any of the other usual women."

"Theodor, what are you leaving out?"

Standing, he paced and said, "She agreed to attend the event with me." He hunched his shoulders. "It was my intention that we would converse about her appointment with me at the office later. Perhaps after the fund-raiser event. But that didn't happen. Before the end of the evening, Tara disappeared, again." He let out a sigh and sat down.

"Let me get this straight. You didn't ask Tara to attend the fund-raiser with you as in a date?"

He nodded his head. "No. Why would I. She had a business appointment scheduled with me. You know I don't mix business with possible clients." His black eyes widened.

Miss Tally blew out a breath. "Sit, but on a whim, on the spare of the moment, while Tara was sitting in your office, you invited her to fill in as your plus one attendee?" Shaking her head, she said, "Tsk-tsk, Theodor, you used that girl. Maybe I should blacken the other eye!" Miss Tally stood; her eyes blazingly locked with his then she tapped his forehead. "Remember, Tara explained she was looking for a soul mate. Hello! And you received her text by mistake."

He removed Miss Tally's boney finger from his forehead and said, "But Tara scheduled a business appointment with me."

"Hum. Now why do you think she came in the office?" She sat down. "Theodor, I can tell you it wasn't for a free consultation in investments."

He tilted his head. "Then what did she want?"

"You need a much-needed time away from work and seriously think why a pretty young thing like Miss Tara Scott wants a serious involvement with a man and why she contacted you. Are you so honestly set in your old bachelor ways you can't see the forest for the tree, tsk-tsk." She walked from the room.

Theodor e-mailed both Kevin and Miss Tally, stating he was out of the office until further notice, and he couldn't be reached. He zipped his computer bag and left the office. He drove to his gated townhouse. Inside, he gathered shorts, jeans, polo shirts, sweatshirt, socks, underwear, hiking boots, cell phone, and a few personal necessities. He opened his nightstand and withdrew his mother's Bible. Within twenty minutes, Theodor was on a mission to be alone.

He traveled toward Logan, Ohio, with music blaring. A sudden fog surrounded him; he flipped the headlights on bright and strained to see the road signs. It was only minutes, but it seemed longer when finally, a sign. The crossroads turning left was Hocking Hill; turn right, Old Man Cave. Theodor decided to continue straight and see what was ahead. After several miles, he saw a narrow road sign that read Hills Cave. Theodor turned left and traveled a thousand foot or so and pulled in to the rustic setting and parked. He entered the lodge and was greeted by a pioneer of a man. "How can we help you, sir? Lost?"

Theodor glanced down at his suit and said, "No, not lost. I would like to rent a cabin. Any available, nothing fancy."

"How long a stay?"

"Three, maybe four days."

"One cabin is available. Cost is $160 a night and $500 deposit up front. There's no refund." The pioneer man stepped behind the counter.

Theodor slipped him his charge card. "How do I reach the cabin?"

"Go pass the lodge until you come to a fork in the road. Stay left until the gravel road ends. The rest of the way is on foot."

He pocketed the receipt and went to the car, picked up his tote and came back inside the lodge. After a change into jeans, polo shirt, and hiking boots, he jammed his suit into the tote. Behind the wheel, the driving became slow and tedious. To add to the fog, large quarter-like raindrops hit the car window and night had set in. Theodor said, "A scene out of a horror story. Glad I'm not superstitious." He placed the car in park at the end of the drivable road and switched off the engine.

Reaching into the glove compartment, he retrieved a flashlight and carefully walked the pathway on foot. It became narrow and slick, but he pushed forward step by step. He heard rushing water sounds to his right. Squinting, he saw the rustic slender shelter. "Home sweet home." Opening the squeaking door, he held the flashlight in hand and saw the room was an open floorplan. A makeshift kitchenette with hotplate and a drip coffeemaker were set on the counter. A woodstove was set in the middle of the floor and a living room surrounded it and a bed set to the left. The cabin provided the bare minimum. He shook his head.

"This isn't a rustic cabin. It's a shed." Theodor carried his computer bag and tote over to the single-sized bed, which would prove to be too small. The pit-a-patt of rain pinged, hitting the tin roof. Raising the flashlight, he saw an oil lantern and, to his surprise, matches. He shuddered. "No bathroom facilities." Theodor opened the heavy door, and sure enough, outside a ways stood an outhouse. He ran.

Throughout the night, he tossed and turned. When he woke, the rains were at a drizzle; the cloud covering cause the sky to be gray. Theodor sat on the bed and ran his hand through his hair. "I wish Dad was here. He loved the outdoors." He read the brochure nature trails formed around the stream. He slid on his hiking boots, grabbed a beef jerky, and headed to the sound of rushing water. Theodor followed a crunched path of grass and watched different birds fly by. He walked for several more hours and was sweaty before finding the stacked canoes. He lifted one to the ground.

Workouts in the gym never gave him the burn his arms and body were feeling. He found a secluded waterfall and anchored the canoe. Theodor shed his boots, shirt, and shorts, down to his navy-blue briefs and dove in. Treading water, he said, "Such a romantic spot with the right woman." Shaking the hair out of his eyes, he watched the falls cascade over the rocks into the water. He climbed on a rock-jutted cliff's edge where daisy flowers emerged and rested.

In the canoe, he shinnied into his shorts and boots and rowed. A few hours later, his stomach growled. Retracing his steps, he lifted the canoe on its stack and pulled a polo shirt on. He was back on the trail that led to the cabin. No food previsions. Glancing at his watch, the hour was near dinnertime. He walked to his car, backed up the narrow path, and in the lodge sought out the diner. Several people were scattered around tables. A fireplace was nuzzled in a corner, not yet with fire, and a piano was softly being played. The tables were lined with white-linen tablecloths. He sat down and viewed the menu. A male waiter said, "Are you ready to order? Would you like coffee?"

He smiled. "Yes to both," He held up his cup, taking a sip, closed his eyes for a moment, then said, "I'll have T-bone steak well done, baked potato, carrots, and house salad with oil and vinegar."

The waiter nodded and left.

He made note to check on fishing rental equipment and best offered spots. The meal arrived, and it was piping hot. He bowed his head. Thoughts of his mother, father, and himself hand in hand around the table and her praying gripped his heart. He couldn't help himself and said a few words of thanks then enjoyed his meal. He tipped the piano player and walked to the front desk. Fishing equipment in hand with a container of night crawlers, he drove to the parking area and walked to the cabin. He lit the oil lamp and got his clothes ready for the next day. He checked his cell phone, no reception. He laughed, brought out his mother's Bible, and read Psalm 23, her favorite, "Comforting," and went to bed. It was another night of interrupted sleep and dreams.

Sitting in the dark, he said, "Time to face why I came to this forsaken camp ground, (a) was it to think, or (b) get away from the grind of year-in-year-out work, or (c) one name came to mind, *Tara*. What was it about her?" With head in hand, he blurted out, "I've dated world-known celebrities, models, and cultural women. Come and go as I please. But Tara is the girl next door, simply beautiful in a 'Doris Day' kind of way, and a little shy, yet she's quite the achiever and survivor. And then there are her enchanting and piercing blue, blue eyes. Oh yes, Tara's a real woman, kind and sincere." He rubbed his eyes, stumbling to the makeshift kitchen and made coffee. Leaning against the counter, he recalled Tara came to his office especially to apologize for not listening to his request for her to stay and get better acquainted at the restaurant. It was confusing. "Yet she hadn't hesitated in accepting the invitation to attend the fund-raiser event. How was I suppose to know she didn't understand that it was not a date, date? Wow, though she was stunning looking!"

He lifted his head, heart heavy. "Tara Scott wants the whole package out of life, the white picket fence, the husband, and the kids." He sat his coffee cup down hard and belted, "No! I'm not the marrying kind of man. I remember how Dad grieved years upon years after Mom died and worked himself to death." Pouring coffee, he sipped the black steaming liquid and glanced out the cabin door. "I'm just fine my way being the bachelor in demand. Love is costly and painful." He reached for the rented fishing gear and worms, heading down the dirt path, whistling.

That evening after a dip in the lake, he made his way back to the lodge. Rain again. He returned the fishing equipment and, being a bit damp, was pleased when he noticed the low burning fire in the fireplace. Only a few dinner people were seated. And the piano man was playing jazz. He moseyed in and ordered his usual meal, crossing his long legs at the ankle to enjoy the roasted coffee served. Upon leaving, the manager flagged him.

"What?"

"Message from a Miss Tally."

# Chapter 8

THEODOR FOLDED THE sealed envelope, tucking it in his back pocket, and walked to the cabin. It was still raining. He lit the oil burner, made coffee, and read the note from Miss Tally.

> It took me long enough to find you, Theodor. Miss Tara Scott made another appointment this time with Kevin Tillman, and she is now his client. She passed her veterinary exam but state board held a twist. She needed to train under a veterinarian for six months for her license to be approved. Her uncle Doug agreed to stay on at the shelter for the remaining six months and will cowork with Tara. Her uncle Doug took employment on Jill's farm, horse training. Which brings me to you, what are you doing in that secluded place, Theodor? Call me, and we'll meet outside of work. I can help you sort out life. Tally.
>
> PS. A sealed envelope arrived yesterday, address to your father, in care of you. It's from the government.

Theodor dropped the note and sipped black coffee. He couldn't surmise why the government had sent a letter. He blew out his coffee. "Hot!"

The sun came breaking through. He chuckled. "Now that I'm leaving."

He pulled on his jeans and a polo shirt, grabbed his tote bag, flashlight, keys, and headed to the car. Stopping off at the lodge, he made his final payment. He thought, *I'll soon be in my business realm.* And head clear, he said, "No room for Tara Scott."

Inside his townhouse, he noticed the nagging green light on the answering machine. Knowing the left, called messages, he rolled his eyes. The shower was steamy hot and felt good. He took a while before shaving and checked out his reflection in the mirror. He noticed his hair was a little long. Smiling on cue and taking a deep breath, he dressed, shaved, and carried a new outlook on his life. It was now showtime, office, and facing Miss Tally.

Whistling and with key in hand, Theodor was surprise to see the office lights on at 5:15 a.m. and hearing Kevin chat with a client. He popped his head around the cubicle, knocking on the frame. "I'm back." His eyes stared at Kevin's client. Theodor blinked, adjusting his shoulders. "Sorry for the interruption." He backed from the cubicle opening, forcing his feet to move. In his office, he shut the door and managed to sit in his chair again head in hands, prayed, "Dear me, its Tara." His phoneline was ringing; Miss Tally appeared. He put a hand in the air. "I know. I should have called you."

She plopped a pod in the coffeemaker, reached for the aspirin bottle, and handed it to Theodor. Next, the coffee. "Drink, 'Columbian' extra roast." She moved a chair closer to her boss. "Theodor, ask Tara out."

He blew out a held breath, roaring, "No, no, no, no!" He absently ran a hand through his black hair. His black eyes almost in slits, he said, "Miss Tally, while at the cabin, I reviewed my life as a boy into manhood. I saw how my mother was the glue that held our family together in her subtle way and in her practicing faith. Now after her death, my father tried to spend time with me and taught me pearls of wisdom, to be educated, and in being my own man." Theodor paced. "I came away with the conclusion that my father grieved himself to death, missing the love of his life, my mother. I watch him work two and three jobs, partly because we needed the money, yet work was his lifeline in the time of grief." He hit the desk. "Life is too short. Look at you." His arms flung open. "You've stayed single, and that's good enough for me." He rose, pinched his nose, and with eyes of steel said, "Now, where's the government letter?" His jaw was set firm and his shoulders straightened.

"Theodor?" She *tsk-tsk* from the office, only to return with a sealed envelope. "Will there be anything else, sir?"

Clearing his throat, he said, "No, no, thank you." His automatic smile was back.

At the door, Miss Tally said, "I'm here for you if you want to talk, Theodor, but I'm sure you're wrong about your father's grief and giving up on life." She quickly closed the door behind her.

He took another sip of strong coffee before he opened the government letter addressed to him. A decorative pin fell to the floor. He reached his fingers down to pick it up, turning it over. Theodor looked back at the letter, which read,

> Sir, we're proud to inform you, Mr. Theodore Welch, that your father, Captain Walter Welch's service information was found and been retrieved. After careful assessment, his military records have been updated. Enclosed you will find 'The Prisoner of War' (POW) award. We are proud to say a retired captain Lucinda Kelt, who served in the military with your father, forwarded Captain Walter Welch's private journal to the headquarters in Washington, DC. She also shared information documented about your father's capture, August 12, 1962, while he was in combat, for the United States military. We appreciate and extend this wonderful opportunity in making your acquaintance at the (POW) Acknowledgement Dinner held at Schmidt's Sausage Haus, 240 E. Kossuth St., Columbus,

Ohio-German Village. This dinner is in the honor of your father and his great sacrifice he made for our country's freedom.

Date: October 10, 2015, Time: 18:00 hours. Please rsvp using the enclosed stamped envelope, guest welcome.

Theodor read the letter again and fingered the pin. He let out a held breath. "I never knew anything about my father's service life. I was just a lad when mother said, 'Your father is on a business trip and would return soon.' She never shared why. It was a long time. And who is Captain Lucinda Kelt my father served with?"

Theodor pushed the call button. "Miss Tally, please step into my office."

"Yes."

Looking down her oversized white-rimmed glasses, Theodor handed her the letter. "I want you to read this. Please sit."

She clutched her chest and sniffled. "Oh, I'm so sorry, but what an honor, a dinner."

Fisting and uncurling his hand, he said, "Find out the proper dress code, confirm the rsvp plus one and call Jeanette, Elisha, or one of the other socialite women for this event. Just let me know who's available. Do see that my plus one receives a fresh bouquet of flowers delivered to her address."

Miss Tally's brown eyes were squinted like slits. She said, "I'll find out the required information and set up your plus one and have flowers delivered." She whisked away with the letter fluttering in her hand, tsk-tsking.

It was nearly lunchtime, and Theodor felt worn out. He had yet to work on his client's e-mails. Theodor stared at the list of e-mails, blew out a breath, and pushed through the compiled list answering e-mails one by one. His stomach growled and his head thumped; the time now was two thirty. Aspirin time, one, two, three and bottled water. He stretched then tilted his head from side to side, shoulder to shoulder. His stomach growled again. He pressed the call button. "Miss Tally, mark me out for a late lunch."

"Are you coming back? Today!"

He scrunched his shoulders and neck to his ears. Hearing Miss Tally's screeching voice explode caused him to silently pour out two more aspirins. He answered, "Yes, in a couple of hours." Theodor pulled his smartphone from his pocket to make a hair-cutting appointment. "What? My stylist has left the salon, permanently, to get married, and you haven't any openings!" He hit the end button and pocketed his cell phone, time for comfy fast food—Wendy's.

A half an hour later, he sat in his BMW hesitating in going back to work. He felt bloated, achy, stressed, and out of sorts, realizing he hadn't shaken his feelings toward the one he wasn't mentioning, Tara. He was in need of a rigid gym workout.

But in the office, hand in slack pocket, he was greeted by Annabelle Chestermeyer with handkerchief in hand dabbing under her eyes. Miss Tally slid between them and handed the unstable woman a glass of water and patted her shoulder.

"See, I told you Mrs. Chestermeyer that Mr. Welch would be right back." She turned facing him with her lips pinched and eyes squinted again. "Come this way, dear. Mr. Welch will see you in the side conference room." She pressed a file in his hand.

Theodor followed behind the two ladies, slowing his steps. Miss Tally stopped abruptly in front of him and said to the hunched-over Annabelle, "I'm sorry for your loss. Your husband seemed like such a good man. He always came in here with a joke." She stepped aside. "Mr. Welch, call me if needed. I'll be at my desk." Her Dr. Scholl pumps clip-clop as she walked away.

He quickly opened the file. A note inside read "Mrs. Chestermeyer wants to liquefy all investments."

"Hello, Mrs. Chestermeyer. What's this I hear about your husband's death? He was a great man and very business smart. I'm so sorry. When did this happen?"

Tears flowed.

He waited and counted to ten, twenty, then thirty.

She spoke, "Mr. Welch, my husband passed away last week, and I think it's best to cash in all our investments."

He stop taking notes and looked up. "Why now?"

Sipping water, she said, "Our attorney informed me that my husband's will has a paragraph that needs sorted out, which means holding up the monthly income. Our checking and savings accounts, bonds, IRA's assets are all froze. How am I to live?"

"I see. Mrs. Chestermeyer, not to sound rude, but your husband received cash from your trust fund's interest check." Theodor rose. "Your husband called me Monday wanting to invest five thousand dollars in varity stock, electricity, and said you would live well off the other ten thousand dollars. Didn't he give you the money?"

She gasps, tears spilled. Slowly breathing in then out, she said, "Tom arrived home Monday from somewhere, muttering something under his breath. He went directly into our bedroom or bathroom, muttering, and then managed to sit in his chair in the TV room. I waved to him as he came through the door for I was busy fixing dinner, and when I went in to tell him dinner was ready, Tom was sitting naturally in his chair with leg crossed over at the ankle and dead."

Theodor reached across his desk, handing Mrs. Chestermeyer the box of Kleenex, and said, "I'm so sorry. I know this must be a shock and a terrible time for you." He straightened in his chair. "But Mrs. Chestermeyer, I need for you to think back for just a moment." He nodded and continued, "Had your husband stayed in his clothes or changed them after he came in the house?"

Mrs. Chestermeyer stared, uncontrollably crying.

Theodor pushed the call button.

Miss Tally glanced at Theodor and then at his client; she shifted, held her smile, and asked, "Tea, anyone?"

Mrs. Chestermeyer sipped her Camellia tea with honey and stated lowly, "Thank you."

Theodor lifted and pulled out a chair for Miss Tally to sit. He came around the desk and squatted down, taking his client's teacup, and placed her hands in his. "Mrs. Chestermyer, let me say again when your husband came in the office Monday, he had a cashier's check in hand for his investment. So"—eyebrow lifted—"he cashed the investment check."

Mrs. Chestermeyer looked pale. "I didn't even know he came into your office. Tom didn't mention a word." Her tears stopped and, staring back, she said, "Are you suggesting I should look around the house for cash?"

He squeezed her hands lightly and nodded. "Did you take the bus in to town?"

"Yes."

"I'll take you home, Mrs. Chestermeyer. Miss Tally and I can help you scout around the house if you would like. And don't worry, we'll decide on your investment decision at a later time." He rose and grabbed his keys.

Miss Tally bunched her lips. "I'll help you, Mrs. Chestermeyer."

Theodor stepped from the office and informed Kevin that he and Miss Tally would be out of the office for most of the day and to call him only if needed. He walked back to his office doorway. "Miss Tally, Mrs. Chestermeyer, my car is parked just outside the building."

Minutes later, he seated Miss Tally in the back and seated Mrs. Chestermeyer in the front passenger seat. He slid behind the wheel and keyed in her address using his smartphone's navigation system.

Half an hour later, in silence, he parked in the client's driveway. Opening the driver's door, he said, "Ladies, wait on me." Arm in arm, they entered the spacious two-bedroom ranch.

Two hours later after searching every room, crack, and cranny, and hearing the lady's cry some more, and finally seeing Thomas's financial files scattered on the floor and not organized, Theodor needed air. He thought about walking outside but darted into the laundry room and cracked open a window. Breathing in and out, he thought, *I'll never get use to death*, and shuttered. He glanced at the Bamboo laundry basket sitting beside the washer, and the only clothes there were a pair of men's slacks and dress shirt. He squatted and checked through the pockets. "Jackpot!" His hands were full of money still wrapped in one hundred dollar bands. Theodor stepped into the hall and motioned for Miss Tally. "Come in here."

"What are you going to do, Theodor? That's way too much money for Mrs. Chestermeyer to have lying around the house, and she can't bank it, tsk-tsk."

He shoved the money in Miss Tally's purse, motioning, shush on her mouth.

Theodor gathered Mrs. Chestermeyer into the front room and sat her down, asking, "Do you have a home safe?"

She shook her head no, paused, and then for the first time, a smile lit her red-rimmed eyes. "Yes!" She pointed to their family portrait hanging on the wall and said, "Slide the frame to the left, Mr. Welch." She bit her bottom lip.

Theodor asked her for the house number again, remembering somewhere he had read birthdates, house numbers, or combinations of phone numbers were used for security codes.

As Mrs. Chestermeyer gave him the numbers, he focused his fingers and turned the dial to the right, stopping on number 11. He did a quick back turn two numbers and stopped on number 9; then he turned the dial completely full circle and stopped on a 7 and then a 5. He twisted and pulled the handle, letting out a healthy sigh.

Mrs. Chestermeyer clapped her hands and on tiptoe looked inside the safe. There were stacks of hundreds dollar bills.

Miss Tally handed Theodor her purse and said, "Annabelle, we found the missing money. Well, Mr. Welch did in the laundry basket in your husband's pant pockets."

"Oh, I forgot, he did change his clothes. That man always picked up after himself."

Theodor said, "Let's put the money in the wall safe."

"Leave out a band of one hundred dollars for me," Mrs. Chestermeyer said.

Theodor did as asked and said, "Mrs. Chestermeyer, does anyone else know about this wall safe, like your attorney, housekeeper, neighbor friend?"

"No! Only you two people."

Theodor closed the safe and slid the portrait in front. "You know there's valuables in the safe: pearls, rings, bobbles, bracelets, necklaces."

She smiled. "It will be our little secret. Wasn't my husband smart?" A giggle slipped. She took Miss Tally's hand, pulling her around and did a happy dance.

Theodor's eyebrows lifted; these ladies were in their late seventies to mideighties. He cleared his throat, covering a chuckle, and asked, "Do you feel safe in your home with just having the silent alarm set?"

"Yes, and I do keep the alarm set." She unexpectedly hugged Theodor at his waist. "Thanks, Mr. Welch." She stepped back. "I'll deal with the attorney later in the week after the funeral." She turned facing Miss Tally and as an afterthought said, "Mr. Welch, we sold our place in Mexico."

He pinched the brim of his nose and said, "Its one less item on your to-do list."

Miss Tally offered, "Dear, if you need someone to accompany you when making the arrangements, I have time coming to me from work." She patted her newfound friend's shoulder. "Call me if you do. Here's my number."

Mrs. Chestermeyer said, "I'll call. And thanks, Cheryl."

Miss Tally nudged Theodor's arm. "We need to check in at the office. Poor Mr. Tillman may need us."

Theodor waited outside for Miss Tally and made her an appointment at the Spring Street Spa. He said, "Miss Tally, an older woman who deserves 'the works' package, bill my office, I'm Theodor Welch."

All the way riding there to the spa, Miss Tally tried to find an excuse for not accepting her boss's spa gift package. But Theodor, not listening, parked his BMW at the curb and walked her to the spa's door. He shoved several bills in her hand and said, "Call a cab when you're finish. I don't want you taking a bus or walking home after dark." As he headed toward his car, he heard that familiar *tsk-tsk*.

He chuckled.

At the office, he noticed it was near closing. Theodor saw Keith at the copier shutting the equipment down. He walked by, nodded, and went inside his office where he checked the calendar schedule and verified his month's travel destinations.

❧⸰⸱❧⸰⸱❧

It began bright and early the next morning. Theodor glanced over at Keith and felt an easiness come over him. He was glad Keith was handling more and more of their clientele's workload. Theodor rejoiced that he could conduct extra seminars, hold motivational speaking engagements, in office and abroad, plus smoothed future clientele.

His path saw very little of Miss Tally, but on necessary occasions, they kept in touch by e-mails, texts, or a phone call. He was thrilled Miss Tally listened and hired two full-time clerks and rode roughshod over them. She was certainly old school, but Miss Tally was also all heart underneath.

❧⸰⸱❧⸰⸱❧

Back from his month's business travel, Theodor hurried into the office and updated investments and added new clientele, signaling Keith. It was almost 4:00 p.m. when Miss Tally popped her head in his office, grinning from ear to ear.

"Remember tonight is the dinner honoring your father. Your date will meet you there at 6:00 p.m. Tuxedo wear, open bar, drinks, mingle, brief introductions, four-course meal, then honorary mention of your father." Twirling, she added, "Possible dancing."

"Miss Tally, who am I escorting?"

Theodor's phone line buzzed. "Hello, just a moment, Miss Tally. Kevin needs you."

"Have fun." She closed his office door.

Now four thirty, Theodor looked for Miss Tally; she was nowhere to be found. He sent a brief e-mail stating he would be out of the office and left. He drove to his gated townhouse and made arrangements for his BMW to be picked up and dropped off after being detailed.

With no time to lose, he selected one of his many black tuxedos, showered, shaved, and added cologne, dressed, and, on final mirror inspection, tucked his invitation plus one card inside his tux's breast pocket, patting it. Theodor smiled after sniffing inside the car. It smelt brand new and fresh.

Theodor drove to the dinner location, anticipating the honoring of his father. A smile filtered across his face as he walked toward the covered door. Inside the foyer, he shifted and stretched his neck looking for his plus one date, thinking, *It's been a while, ole boy, since being seen out on the town.*

He gave his name to the hostess, adding there will be a plus one, and bolstered up his prize smile. She checked his name off the list and asked him to step aside. Glancing at his Rolex watch, he noticed it was ten after 6:00 p.m. He thought, *My socialite women were never late to a function.* He texted Miss Tally, "Who's my plus one?"

"Mr. Theodor Welch?" a man from behind asked.

Nodding, he raised his hand and said, "Yes."

A message was handed to him coming from Miss Tally. "Go ahead and mingle. Your date will soon be arriving. Again such a special night relax and enjoy the honor." *Strange woman that Miss Tally*, Theodor thought.

A man in uniform touched his shoulder. "Step this way, Mr. Welch, someone will assist you at the open bar."

# Chapter 9

JILL PRICE CALLED Miss Tally and made an appointment with just her. They had become acquainted and friends before Theodor Welch had taken over the business of Edwin Jays Investments. On Saturday, Miss Tally usually didn't work, but she was at the office waiting to hear the gossip from Jill. The overhead bell dinged. Miss tally said, "We shouldn't be bothered this morning, neither Kevin Tillman, our new financial advisor, nor Mr. Welch are scheduled in the office." She handed Jill a strong black coffee. "So what's the juicy story on Tara Scott?"

Jill sipped several times before sitting her coffee cup on the desk and scooted forward. "Well, let me say that sweet girl only wants a real homebody man to love, and she's all messed up in her thinking about Theodor."

Miss Tally licked her lips. "Really? I've seen her, but what's she like, Jill?"

"Tara's just a little thing. Couldn't weigh hundred pounds soak and wet. She dresses somewhat artsy. Her long red hair looks like a burning fire, and her large blue eyes makes you want to hug her. You know she doesn't have a single soul to look after her except that wonderful uncle of hers that's recently came to town. He's working at the animal shelter as a veterinarian. But he's another story." She blew out a held breath, fanning her pinkened face with a cowboy hat.

"Jill?" Looking over her white-rimmed glasses, she screeched, "Something's going on between you and that cowboy?"

"Now, Miss Tally, I came in here to give you the scoop on poor lost in love Tara Scott." Taking another sip of coffee, she continued, "A few days ago, her uncle called me and made arrangements for Tara to come to the farm using a horseride for us women to talk.

"After several hours and nothing, I suggested we rest our horses. Tara slid from the horse, and the tears turned into sobs until her whole body shook. It was hard to watch and wait for her to calm down. Finally, between jags of tears, Tara managed to say how she went on the Internet and checked out a dating site. She found a man of interest and immediately sent him a text for a meet up, but unknown to her, the text went to Theodor Welch's phone instead. Tara later discovered she had typed in the wrong number by one digit. She and Theodor met after a few texts took place, and she implied how nice, patient, polite, and handsome he was.

"When Tara finally realized her error in the text, she made an appointment to confront him. However, she didn't get to completely explain, for she was interrupted when he received a phone call in his office."

Leaning in, Miss Tally said, "Can you believe this hot mess. Oh that poor girl only wanting love, and she meets Mr. Uncongenial all business mode man, Theodor. Tsk-tsk."

Jill said, "Did you know he asked her to attend a fund-raiser and another woman confronted her that same evening with a chilly phrase and then kissed Mr. Welch. Needless to say, Tara was confused and left the fund-raiser after she called her uncle to come pick her up."

Jill stood for a moment then sat back down and drank the rest of her coffee. "That Theodor sniffed around Tara's house in the wee hours after he discovered she was gone from the fund-raiser, and he got a surprise meeting up with the wrath of her uncle Doug's right hook."

"Well, Jill. They can have another chance meeting, Tonight, Friday." Jill's eyebrows rose. "Theodor is attending a military formal dinner honoring his late father. He's to have a significant plus one too attend with him." Scooting closer to Jill in almost a whisper, Miss Tally said, "How do we pull this meeting fate off? And how do we get the uncle on board?"

Jill let a giggle slip. "Don't worry about Doug. I'll take care of him. But Tara I don't have a clue."

"We need her dress size and shoe size. We need to dazzle her and hit her emotional side pertaining to Theodor to get her to accept the invitation."

Jill's brown eyes widened. "What about our never marrying Theodor? Doesn't he have a say?"

"Tsk-tsk. He's so over the moon with Tara he doesn't know when to come in out of the rain. He's like a fighting bull." Miss Tally stood and refreshed their coffee. "Let's see"—tapping her cup—"Jill, call that perky receptionist at the shelter and do your thing having her to believe it's her idea to take Tara shopping for the formal wear. Maybe offering her a gift card?"

"Miss Tally, you're a dog's tail. All right, I'm in."

"Okay. I'll make an appointment for Tara to come into the office and be convincing so she attends the honored dinner. I'll paint Theodor as a sad-stricken soul having a tough time with his grief and perhaps he could find closure for his late father. Of course I'll swear her to secrecy that we never spoke or that she's aware of his hidden sadness, and I'll make sure she knows not to share anything with him at any cost." She smiled.

Jill said, "So if Mr. Uppity babbles hurtful words are said to Tara, she will think he's just hurting from the lost. Oh, Miss Tally, you're a genius." Jill hugged Miss Tally and saw herself to the door.

Miss Tally called out, "We'll touch base on our plan."

━━❖━━

Friday by midafternoon, the receptionist placed the lunch sign in the animal shelter's window and all but shoved Tara out the door with Uncle Doug driving them to Tuttle Mall.

Tara said, "Why am I going shopping?"

The woman looked at Tara's uncle. He said, "Your wardrobe is lacking, and the stores are all having 50 to 75 percent off sale today. Jill called me. She just came from there. You need after-five wear, hose, dress shoes, and our receptionist has quite the flair." He smiled. "Remember that red dress?"

Uncle Doug parked the truck and shoved monies into Tara's hand. "Now take this and buy you some nice things, call it your graduation gift." He smiled, saying, "Mary Beth, here's a little something for you. We appreciate how hard you've worked at the shelter while Tara's been busy studying. What's this I hear you've been offered another position as Tara's CSR? Great news."

"Come on, Uncle Doug!"

Holding up a hand, Uncle Doug said, "Tara, Mary Beth, we'll meet up at the truck." Checking his watch, he continued, "Two o'clock. I'm moseying over to the leather shop. I understand they have a display of saddles." He tilted his cowboy hat, and a deep smile appeared.

Mary Beth said, "Your uncle is a good-looking man, yummy for his age. Hurry, Tara, we don't want to miss a sale." She looped arms with Tara and all but ran into the first store.

Uncle Doug went on into the leather shop and saw a saddle he hunkered for. He spoke with the salesperson and blew out a sigh then said, "Get the manager!"

The salesperson hunched and hurried away.

Reaching a hand out, the store manager said, "Hello, I'm Pete Wade, how may I help you?"

After a hardy shake, Doug said, "What can you tell me about that saddle"—he pointed—"Mr. Wade?"

Mr. Wade chuckled. "It's expensive compared to other saddles we have in the store, but the leather is smooth. The Billy Royal Training Saddle offers easy break in and maintenance. I have requests of this saddle from the Spanish and Arabian horse breeders." He touched the saddle, emphasizing the softness. Pete stepped closer to Doug and almost in a whisper said, "My new salesperson meant no harm, and he should not have assumed the saddle's cost was too much. Sir, is this saddle the one you've been looking for?"

Doug liked Pete's attitude. "I'll take it."

The time passed quickly, Mary Beth and Tara giggled, while pushing a loaded cart carrying their packages to the truck.

"Buy out the store?" Doug shifted his hat and helped placed their packages in the back of his truck, moving his boxed saddle. His cell phone rang. "Hello, Doug here." His lips lifted. "Sure, I can do that, and that."

Tara said, "Uncle Doug, you're a man of few words," and she giggled more.

"Mary Beth, I'm dropping you off at the shelter to relieve Jill—ah, Miss Price, and, Tara, we'll swing by your place and drop off the packages before heading into town."

The ladies looked at each other and settled back in their seat.

At the shelter, Jill explained to Mary Beth the incoming phone calls then slipped from behind the counter, smiling from ear to ear. Doug climbed down from the truck and helped Jill up; his eyes were shielded by his hat.

Tara, Jill, and Doug carried packages into Tara's house and, of course, was greeted by Snow. Tara softly gave a command, and

Snow dropped to the floor. Tara began opening the sacks and was stopped. Jill said, "You've met Miss Tally before, right?"

"Yes," Tara said, lips bunched.

"She's waiting at the office and needs to talk with you." Raising a hand, she continued, "It's a private matter concerning Theodor Welch."

"What, we've nothing to talk about!"

Jill glanced at Doug. Doug said, "Listen, I don't like that man any more than you do, Tara, but Miss Tally is a pillar in the community and requested to see you. It could be of importance. I'll drive."

Tara said, "I want to…"

Uncle Doug and Jill were herding her out to the truck. Doug lifted Tara and placed her in the seat. "Buckle up."

Jill said, "I'll stay here and let Snow out and hang up your stuff. Go."

Driving toward Columbus, Tara belted out, "What on earth is going on?" She turned and looked narrowly at her uncle Doug. He was whistling.

He stopped in front of the massive building and put his truck into park. "Tara, I'm heading back to the shelter. Call me if you need a ride home." Then he stared straight ahead and said, "Mr. Welch has done okay in life."

Tara shook her head and walked into the building and saw her uncle leave.

⊱⋅ ⊰

"Hello, my dear, so glad you could make it into the office today. Here, let's go into the conference room." Miss Tally smiled. "Coffee or tea, Tara?"

Tara shook her head but said, "Coffee's fine, black."

A few minutes later, Tara was handed a mocha latte, and Miss Tally fluffed her handkerchief in the air. "I know my asking you here today appears strange, but poor Theodor." She peeked over her handkerchief. "May I swear you to secrecy?"

Tara scooted closer to Miss Tally for her voice was extremely hushed. Tara lifted her cup and, a few sips later, sat her cup down placing her hands in her lap. "Go on, Miss Tally. Whatever you tell me will remain in this room between us."

"Well, dear child, read this letter first and then again." Miss Tally blew her nose and poured a tea.

"Theodor's father was captured?" She strained toward Miss Tally. "There's a dinner in his honor tonight. Wow!"

Miss Tally nodded and scooted her chair in closer. The women were almost head to head. "I really shouldn't say anything, but our Theodor." She looked over her white wide-rimmed glasses. "But when Mr. Welch finally realized your text to him was a mistake, he was disappointed somewhat because it was not business. However, he admitted to me he finds you attractive. God's Word." She touched Tara's lips. "Just listen. His mother died when he was eleven years old and his father raised him. They weren't poor, poor, but life wasn't easy either. His father worked three jobs to see that his son was educated." She passed the Kleenex to Tara and patted her shoulder and stood. "You see, Tara, Theodor mistook his father's work in making a better life for him as in a man who was grief stricken, which led to his father's early death."

"But I don't understand what all this has to do with me."

Miss Tally said, "Let me make myself perfectly clear then. Theodor blames himself because his mother died at such a young age. He thought if only he had helped out more at home. And he perceives his father's work was a direct release from the loss of his wife. And when Theodor turned eighteen, his father died. He's without family. That's why I've stayed on here for so long. Theodor married his work from that day on so no one could make him feel and be vulnerable in a real woman's relationship." She sat Tara's and her cups on the counter.

"So?" Tara asked, arms wide open.

"As I mentioned, our Theodor has feelings for you, Tara." She took her hands in hers. "He told me so, but he's also confused and a very stubborn man. Tonight, as I said, is the honorary dinner, and he needs a plus one. And if you have any feelings for him or think he's worth the fight to win your man, then here is your plus one ticket. It's a formal affair." She moved toward the closed door.

"It's ten minutes before five o'clock, and the dinner is at six. I'll never make it in time, Miss Tally."

"You go home get dress and let me make the arrangements. I'll have your uncle drive you to the event, but under no circumstances is Theodor to know what we've spoken about! Can you handle that?"

Doug was waiting outside the building. Tara shook her head and stepped up into the truck. "You all right, girl?"

"Uncle Doug, do you know about self-made Mr. Welch?"

"Enough. I just don't want you to get hurt."

They rode in silence to her house.

Jill greeted Tara and motioned her to hurry. "Grab your shower. I'll have your evening gown waiting then Mary Beth can arrange your hair and don't get your makeover face wet."

Tara giggled and saluted.

At the restaurant door, Tara inhaled a deep breath, willing calmness to her nerves.

It was now six twenty and the bar was open. She was quickly escorted to the bar and spotted Theodor at the other end. She picked up a bubbly flute and prayed, "I need Your help." She tasted a liquid sip and licked her red lips. He turned, and his dark eyes flickered. He observed her from head to toe and then slowly walked toward her. She smoothed the long form-fitting black dress with a thigh slit.

His eyes twinkled. "Are you my plus one tonight?" Smiling, he thought of Miss Tally.

She forced a smile and countered, "Yes. Hope you're not too disappointed."

He placed his hand low on Tara's back and paused; their eyes locked, and his black eyes darkened. He leaned in, and his breath tickled her neck; she shuttered and felt warm.

"No, I'm not in the least disenchanted." His finger touched her lips. "You take my breath away. Tara Scott, you're beautiful." He leaned in and ever so lightly brushed her lips then straightened.

She felt the heat tracking from neck to face. But she batted her blue eyes and said, "Why thank you, Theodor, and may I add you scrub up real nice."

He threw his head back and laughed. Their names were called. At the dinner table, he seated her and whispered, "There's dancing tonight."

She shivered and silently admired his broad shoulders and his gorgeous, perfect face. Yes, she was more than attracted to him; she was falling fast and hard.

The waiter in white gloves served their house salad then asked their choice of pea soup or French onion sprinkled with shredded cheese. Her half-filled bubbly flute was replaced. His coffee cup filled. The waiter arrived with steaming sausage stuffed with croute. Afterward, apple strudel desert came with vanilla ice cream. She could hold no more, excusing herself; he stood, and she felt his eyes on her back. Tara realized power and swayed her hips, giggling.

The table was cleared when she returned. He again, being a gentleman, seated her.

His fingers lingered on her right bare shoulder, and she felt a sizzle down her entire body. She must remind him hands off. Just then, Theodor was called up front and handed a folded American flag. Words concerning his honored father were given, filled with strength, wisdom, and purity. And clapped hugs on the back.

A mature older woman was wheeled where Theodor stood, and they were introduced. "Captain Lucinda Kelt, meet your friend Captain Walter Welch's son, Mr. Theodor Welch." They shook hands, and Theodor leaned down thanking her for her part in his father's award ceremony dinner. He kissed her cheek and a tear slid down. Tara saw his strong chiseled jaw twitch. She saw his eyes held so much tenderness as he glanced her way. Her heart plummeted. He nodded and came back to the table, and his eyes were as steel, cold. Tara thought, *He could change his mood on a dime. Maybe I don't want to be a part of his life.*

He touched her arm. "Tara?" Maybe he was weighing his words. This wasn't easy for either of them. He nodded and looked a little too long. "May I have this dance?"

She touched her flawless upsweep and rose. In a whisper, she said, "I'd love to."

He was proper in his hold, but heat penetrated through their touch, smile, and eyes. She melted into him, and he led dance after dance.

He bent his head and brushed her lips, saying, "Thank you, plus one," then lifted his head and tipped her backward.

His face showed strength and desire flashed from his darkened eyes. The music stopped; she blew out a heated breath, glancing at her watch like Cinderella. It was past time for her to leave. She whispered in his ear, "Uncle Doug's waiting for me outside. Thanks for tonight, and what a tribute to your father."

⊱✦⊰

Doug watched as his niece all but waltzed to the truck. He jumped down and notice Theodor Welch was a few steps behind Tara walking toward him.

"Sir, thank you for bringing Tara tonight and allowing her to be my plus one. It's a night I'll never forget for your act of kindness."

Doug nodded when Theodor placed a hand on his forearm. He tensed. Theodor privately said, "I would like to see Miss Tara Scott again. May I call on her tomorrow afternoon?"

"No!" He lifted his cowboy hat and walked toward Tara then stopped and turned, muttering, "You can join us at Ms. Jill Price's farm tomorrow, say, two thirty for late lunch."

Theodor sidestepped and let out a held breath. "Yes sir, thank you. I'll be there." He stood to Tara's side of the truck. "May I help you up?"

She missed a stepped, and Theodor reached out and caught her arm and lifted her as a leaf into the truck. Leaning in, he said, "I'll see you tomorrow." He kissed her hand and shut the door.

Tara leaned over and kissed Doug's cheek. He listened to the truck's music as he drove. All eyes were straight ahead.

# Chapter 10

JILL PACED BACK and forth in her large kitchen after hanging up the phone from Doug. She had planned on Doug and Tara for dinner, but now there would be an added uppity scale Theodor. She said, "I guess it's only fair to Miss Tally and what I've put Doug through to at least see for myself if there's any solidness in Theodor when it comes to a woman. Well, pot roast it is." Out came the vegetables, potatoes, onions, and carrots. She used her trusty peeler and set to work skinning their surfaces. The shoulder roast was seasoned and placed in the old iron skillet. While waiting for it to brown, Jill heard the oven timer bell ding. With pot holders in hand, she removed her prize-winning apple pie and sat it on the windowsill to cool. Jill flipped the roast over and let the sizzling juices take over. She cut the flame down and began chopping the vegetables smaller and lifted the iron skillet's lid to add the vegetables around the meat. Jill took a whiff. "Smelling good!" Some water was added, thyme, extra salt, and pepper. She placed the large-covered skillet in the oven and set the timer for one hour and knew when it dinged to add more time.

Half an hour later, her doorbell chimed. Jill glanced into the hall mirror and touched her neatly cropped hair and pinched her cheeks. With smile, Jill opened the door. Theodor had arrived in with, of course, a business suit and silk tie. "Come in. The others haven't arrived yet."

She was handed a beautiful arrangement of wild flowers, and her brown eyes widened as Theodor kissed her cheek. "Thank you, Theodor. They're lovely." He has not only charm but also manners; Jill smiled as they walked into the large eat-in kitchen. She served him black coffee and checked the oven, setting the timer again. The door chimes rang.

Jill turned to open the door, and Theodor had followed behind her. Doug nodded and removed his boots and placed his Stetson hat on the foyer's hook. He brought forward a picked bouquet of fresh mixed flowers and handed them to Jill. Pulling her in closer and bending, he lightly brushed Jill's lips.

"Well, thank you, cowboy." Her neck to face was heated. She fluffed her apron.

Tara, still in the doorway, nodded at Theodor and stepped inside so the door would shut. Her uncle reached out his arms and said, "Ladies?" They walked into the kitchen, and Theodor followed. Tara looked over her shoulder and thought, *Doesn't he look just like a lost puppy dog.* She dropped arms. "Jill, what do you want me to do?"

Theodor stepped beside Tara. "May I help?"

Jill said, "Tara, while the tea is brewing, please have Theodor squeeze the lemonades and you make the lemonade for later." And with hands on her plump hips, she caught Doug's eye. He stepped forward, and Jill whispered, "Go out to the barn and see if one of the cowhands has something Mr. GQ can slip into, mercy me." She fanned herself. "In a suit on the farm."

Doug chuckled. A few minutes later, Doug touched Theodor's arm. "Follow me."

At the barn, Theodor removed his initial handkerchief from his front pocket and whipped at his shoes. Doug doubled over laughing. "Man, are you out of your element." He handed him a handful of clean straw. "Watch your step."

Theodor shook his head when a cowpoke smirkingly said, "These should fit. Go inside the stall and change."

Doug, still chuckling, straightened and sobered as Theodor rounded the stall. "Now you look like you belong, boots and all." He placed a hand on his shoulder. "Do you know how to ride a horse?"

Theodor blew out a held breath. "Some. Not really my forte!"

"You need to understand Tara's a country gal. She loves working with animals and is quite good at what she does." Doug tightened his grip. "Don't hurt Tara. If you can't accept her lifestyle and if you don't picture her in your future, move on with your shakers and movers in your high society world. She needs a real man's man." He dropped his hand and moved from the barn.

The table was set, and Doug held the chair for Jill then Tara. Jill reached her hands out, and Doug, Tara, and finally Theodor clasped hands. Jill said a brief prayer of thanks for the food and company. The roast was passed around followed by the bowl of vegetables and homemade bread. The iced tea was smoothing. Doug rose to help Jill with the pie.

Theodor and Tara made small talk; then she said, "Your acquired clothes become you as well as your business suits." Her blue eyes sparkled.

"Well, these are borrowed as you know. I understand we're going horseback riding." He blew out a breath. "Like your uncle said, I'm out of my element here. I'm sorry. I really don't know how to just relax. Maybe I should just go."

Tara's eyes narrowed, and she bit on her bottom lip.

Jill stood smiling while Doug handed each person their large sliver of apple pie with ice cream. Nods and oohs and aahs were said.

Tara motioned Theodor to come over to the sink. He carried his plates and silverware. Dishes were washed, rinsed, and Theodor dried and placed them in their spots.

Doug and Jill slipped outside. They saddled the horses after Doug unloaded his newest saddle. Jill lifted her eyes, but Doug hunched his shoulders. "What? I want to be comfortable working with the Arabian. It's nothing."

Before entering the house, Jill, on tiptoe, kissed Doug. "You're quite the cowboy!"

His side smile lifted; he lowered his hat, taking a step back from Jill, whispering, "You're quite the woman."

She reached for his hand, and he entwined his fingers with hers. He muttered, "I've been hog-tied and now branded."

She only squeezed his hand harder and blushingly smiled.

Tara and Theodor burst through the front door and waited for their loaned horse. As the four rode in the meadows, Doug said, "Where'd you learn to ride, Theodor?"

With reins in hand and a little heel side kick to the horse, he said, "My father sent me to summer camp while growing up. Their specialty was in horses." He glanced Tara's way. "It was a long time ago, almost a forgotten era."

Several hours later, they rested the horses and them. Jill pointed to the saddlebags while spreading a blanket. Doug opened the pouches and pulled out refreshments, lemonade, PJ's sandwiches, and sliced carrot sticks.

"Theodor, how was the honorary dinner for your father?" Jill asked.

"It was enlightening. Nice words were spoken in regard to my father and his service to our nation. I met the captain responsible for the tribute to my father, Captain Lucinda Kelt, a warm person." He reached for Tara's hand. "And I was gifted with a surprise plus one, and can she dance."

The serious mood was broken when Jill and Doug chuckled, but Tara's face pinkened; then a giggle slipped. After a stretch, Doug stood and helped clean up the refreshments. Jill folded the cloth, and everything was neatly packed into the saddle pouches. They traveled the trail back to the barn. Each one had the duty to rub down their horse.

Theodor suddenly realized he hadn't thought of clients or work relativeness all day. His mind had been focused on Tara Scott. His heart beat faster and perspiration beaded on his forehead. Theodor quickly bid all a farewell and said, "I'll return the clothes." And turning to Tara. "I'll call you when I'm back in town." In his car, he could hardly breathe; anxiety and fear set in as he realized his genuine caring feelings for Tara. "No, I'm not the forever kind of man. Couldn't happen." He barreled done the lane, dirt flying.

⋅⋗⧖⧑⋖⋅

Doug stepped over to Tara and wrapped his arm around her waist, fisting his other hand. Tara patted his hand. "Uncle Doug, mind if I take your truck back to the shelter? I need to check on the two new felines that came in last night. They're both expecting, and by the looks of things, it may be anytime."

Jill offered, "He can use the old farm truck later."

He nodded and tossed the keys to his niece.

⋅⋗⧖⧑⋖⋅

She held tight to the wheel, forcing the tears back. She said, "From now on, I'm focusing my time on my work. No more Mr. Theodor Welch. He's complicated, perhaps a lost cause." Tears threatened. She slammed the truck door harder than necessary but didn't let a single tear drop.

Inside the shelter's clinic area, dogs were howling, cats were hissing, and the two mommy cats to be were in a stretch, moaning. It was happening. "I wish Uncle Doug was here!"

⋅⋗⧖⧑⋖⋅

"Hey, Tara. Let's do this," Doug said. He walked to the sink, held his hands under the faucet, and the hot water started, "Scrub up, girl."

"You almost beat me here. Thanks." She tapped the powder on his hands and hers and snapped, gloves were in place. Both Tara and Doug were on mommy-to-be cat standby.

Doug mentioned, "I couldn't get the cats off my mind, they seemed so skittish before I left the shelter earlier, and through dinner and horseback riding. Then afterward, you gave me the vibe of personal unsettlement." He held the cream-colored cat and motioned to the antiseptic. "Get the mask!"

Just then, the gray-and-white calico cat moaned louder. Tara nodded and let Doug deal with the sedated cream-colored cat. She went on to the gray-and-white calico cat. Delivery had begun. An hour later, five gray felines were born. The mommy cat screeched again, and Tara did a quick little slit for the male kitten marked just like the momma to be born.

Doug rushed over and placed a cloth under the mommy's nose. He lifted her like fresh eggs and set her in a sterile cage with her babies. Then he darted back to the cream-colored cat named Butter and snapped on new gloves. She was birthing slowly, only two baby males were delivered. Tara said, "That was a rush. Glad you were here."

He nodded, "I'll do the watch tonight," and growled, "Why don't you head on home and take a long bubble bath and wash that man out of your hair."

She raised a hand. "Uncle Doug, Theodor is a fine man. He just has a lot to deal with."

"Ya, like grow up!"

She squeezed his arm and plopped a kiss on his cheek. "I think I'll take your first advice and take a hot bath. Can you drop me off at home or may I take your truck?"

"I'll call Jill. I'm sure she's all right with me having the farm truck tonight. Take my truck and be careful. See you tomorrow, right, church?"

Tara batted her eyes in the surprise answer that her uncle gave—church—but kept her mouth closed and nodded.

The tub was soon filled with hot bubbly fragrant water where Tara slid down, emerging her shoulders and closing her eyes. When the water began cooling, she used her toes, and the hot water trickled on. Tara's thoughts were all jumbled. *Theodor came across like hot and cold water. One time he would be adoring and affectionate, and the next time cool and distant, sending out very mix signals.* "I need to move forward with my life and let him do the same." Tara pulled the tub's plug, cleaned the sides and bottom of the tub, stepped out, and towel dried. She slid into her old sweats and went into the living room and snuggled on the sofa with Snow.

She woke alarmed to the dinging of her doorbell and Snow barking. She blinked. "What time is it anyway?" She stumbled to the front door where someone was now pounding and dinging the bell again. "Hold your horses." Tara peeked out the front window, and Theodor's BMW was parked beside her uncle's truck. She flung the door open. "Do you know what time it is? Well, I do. It's four thirty in the morning!" she barked, placing her hand on her hips.

He stepped forward. "Doug here?" he asked, looking over Tara's shoulder and absently rubbing his jaw.

"No, not at the moment. Why?" she answered, still not moving.

Theodor ran a hand through his tousled hair. "Tara, you're driving me crazy." He grabbed her and drew her near and, bending his head, gave her a hard warm kiss. He edged closer, probing her lips with his tongue.

Tara stepped back and slapped his face. "Just what do you think you're doing? You left me, remember?" She narrowed her blue eyes. "You're tighter than a hinged door, and I'm not going to be a part of your confusion." She tempted to close the door. "Move your foot! Go on down the road with your unattached, unemotional playboy ways. As for me, I'm not a shaker and mover kind of gal."

His mouth gaped.

"I'll be in church where I'll pray for you. Now get out, leave me alone. So you know, online Timothy reached out to me through a text, so…"

"Tara, don't."

Door only inches from his face, she said, "Don't what? Want a life with someone that's wants to commit and be with me? Ha! Go." She slammed the door and leaned against it. Her knees were knocking and her heart beat faster. Tara listened, and, finally, his car motor purred and then it riveted. His tires squealed, and Theodor was gone. At last she was alone; the house was too quiet even with Snow's whimper. Tara made her decision to what? Go to confession because she lied. There could be no Timothy. She held her sides. There would be no crying. Tara felt numb.

Gathered at the community church, Marybeth waved Jill and Doug up front. Tara slid in, and the man directing the music asked the congregation to stand. Doug held a song book out in front of him and his base voice filled the room. Jill's off-keyed voice belted with his. Marybeth sang alto and Tara soprano. They were a strange collective group, but a bond brought them together through faith, friendship, and, yes, strangely love.

The minister read from James and spoke on brotherly love. Tara squirmed. All met at Jill's for dinner and helped with the chores. The trucks were exchanged, and Mary Beth gave Tara a ride into the shop. She unlocked the door to the clinic and checked on the momma cats and their babies. A lot of meowing was heard. Both mommas were lying content with their offspring.

Fresh water and food was set out. A few kind words were spoken and handling of the kittens and cats. Tara asked, "Mary Beth, would you mind taking me home?"

In the car, Mary Beth said, "I'm dying to hear how the honorary dinner went with Mr. Dreamy." Her green eyes widened.

Tara stared straight ahead. "That night was magical. You were right about the black dress." She turned and looked at Mary Beth. "We held hands. He placed an arm around me and asked me to dance and no one else existed. But when the evening came to close, Uncle Doug came to take me home." She yawned. "However, Theodor asked Doug if he could date me. It was touch and go for a while, and I held my breath. Doug first said no then agreed that Theodor could come to dinner at Jill's the next afternoon and go horseback riding."

"What happened? Are you two dating?" Mary Beth rubbed her hands together. "Did he feel the connection with you as Miss Tally and Jill mention?"

Mary Beth parked in Tara's driveway.

Tara cracked her door open and turned. "Unfortunately, there were moments of real connection. You know Theodor can date anyone in the world. He's so polished, and I'm more country. We seem to have different cultural interests. I guess the sparks just weren't electric enough for him." She hunched her shoulders and sniffed. "See you at work tomorrow." She waved her new friend on.

Snow settled in front of the lit fireplace. Tara's eyes were drifting close. She settled into the couch and pulled the cover over her. She faded in and out of sleep. Her head ached and pounded more when the house phone rang. "Hello?"

"Tara, it's me, Miss Tally. I'm sorry to call so late, but I couldn't wait any longer. Are you all right?"

"Yes, Miss Tally, but I was trying to sleep. I have an early day tomorrow. Why do you ask?" She sat up now; her eyes were wide open.

"Well, the last I heard, Theodor indicated he had a nice evening with you and was pleased you were his plus one and was happy that Doug agreed in him seeing you at Jill's farm. So what happened?"

"Not to be rude, Miss Tally, but Theodor doesn't want any kind of commitment with a woman. He's happy man living the bachelor's life."

She only heard Miss Tally's rush breathing. "Sorry, dear, to have wakened you. I'll try and find Theodor."

"Why, did he disappear?"

"He has. I haven't anything scheduled for him in town or out of state or country. I had hoped he was with you. Theodor hasn't answered any of my e-mails, texts, or phone calls. I'm worried about him. This is so unusual for him." She sniffled. "I called the police after I called his colorful women, and the police said I have to wait twenty-four hours before filing out a missing person's report."

# Chapter 11

TARA'S MOUTH GAPED wider. Theodor Welch was now missing. Was it her fault she hadn't been willing to listen to him or even try to communicate? She'd just thrown him out on his ear. "Well, what am I to do now?" she asked, blowing out a breath. Tara couldn't sleep after rolling and tossing. She called Doug,

On the third ring, a groggy Doug said, "Hello, Tara gal, are you all right?"

She was crying loudly and no words spelt forward. Doug said, "I'll be right there after I pick up Jill. She's coming with me."

The doorbell rang. Tara opened the door still sniffling. Miss Tally stepped in and said, "Jill called and asked me to meet her here. Oh dear, you're so upset. Show me to your kitchen, and I'll make us a pot of tea." She placed a hand on Tara's arm and was led to the kitchen. Miss Tally turned the fire on under the teakettle and waited for the water to boil. The front doorbell dinged, and Miss Tally motioned Tara to stay seated. She shuffled to the door and motioned Jill and Doug in. She said, "Tara's in the kitchen, she's a mess. We were about to have a cup of Camellia tea."

Doug nodded and kept walking. Tara flew into his strong arms and threw up.

Jill rushed through the house gathering towels and a washcloth. Tara was shivering. Jill led her to the bathroom with the cup of tea and turned on the shower. "Come on, slid out of your clothes and step into the shower. We'll talk afterward," Jill said. She collected the soiled clothes and loaded the washing machine, calling out to Doug, "Cowboy, please come here."

"Coming." He went to his truck and retrieved a wrinkled Cranbury shirt, slipping it on.

Jill tended the wash until everything was cleaned and dried. Miss Tally twisted her hands and paced back and forth. Her cell phone rang, she jumped. "Hello?"

"Miss Tally, this is Georgette, an old acquaintance of Theodor Welch."

"I know who you are. Tsk-tsk. Woman, why are you calling me back?"

"I thought you should be notified."

"Why? Do you know Theodor's whereabouts?" Miss Tally motioned to Doug and Jill to sit with Tara. She continued, "And is he all right? I've been out of my mind with worry! Just why didn't he call me?" She put the cell phone on speaker.

"Miss Tally, please calm down and let me speak. I came unannounced to Aspen to visit with my father and two brothers. I'd hoped to skiing and to meet someone. I was surprised beyond words to see my old friend, Theodor."

"He's what? Tsk-tsk. On a skiing trip? That wasn't on his schedule. He just went there out of the blue. Put him on the phone now."

"Sorry, Miss Tally, please hear me out. I'm not the enemy." She blew a breath then said, "My father called the trained rescue team when Theodor became missing. They found Theodor and his cell phone in a snowbank and notified my father. See, Theodor was with him on this trip. I overheard them tell Father that a Miss Tally needed to be called. She's his contact person."

"What?"

"Miss Tally, Theodor needs surgery. His left leg is broken in three places. The rescue team said he lost his balance on the ski slope when an unexpected snowstorm blew in. It caused a complete whiteout. I'm losing signal." Silence.

Miss Tally held the buzzing receiver in her hand and screeched, "Oh no, poor Mr.

Welch." She began sniffling and stumbled to a chair.

Doug removed the receiver from her hand and hung up the phone. He braced Miss Tally sitting her down. Doug said, "Jill, why don't you pour Miss Tally a tea."

And in came Tara wearing a terry cloth robe and fluffy slippers. She said, "What happened?"

Miss Tally blew her nose on her handkerchief, took a sip of hot tea, and cried, "Our Theodor must have had been called to Aspen on business. The caller stated he was on a ski slope with clients when a complete snow whiteout happened from unexpected whipping winds." She blew her nose again. "He's now in the hospital needing surgery on his leg."

The kitchen pack of women sounded like bees swarming in a beehive. Doug said, "Miss Tally, would you like me to fly to Aspen and see to Mr. Welch and his arrangements in getting him home. I'm familiar with Aspen, spent some time there healing after my bull encounter, and I've skied myself in the day."

Jill touched Miss Tara's shoulder. "Now now, we'll figure something out."

Doug's eyes searched her brown eyes and lingered. "Yes, there's always a solution."

Tara busted out loud, "This is my entire fault. Theodor came to my house in the wee hours, kissed me, and told me he was crazy about me." She shivered. "I slapped him and demanded he go. I said some awful things to him." Tears were blinked back. "I didn't listen to him. I prejudged his no commitment self."

Jill gathered Tara in her arms, and Miss Tally said, "Oh dear, you're not at fault. I'm the one who's encouraged him toward you."

Doug, in his thunderous base voice, said, "Theodor is a grown man who I believe is wavering as a bachelor. I suppose he understands that his single days are numbered, and he's scared. My niece is different in a good way from those women he knows." He glanced directly at Jill and locked eyes with her.

As if she knew he was applying himself in the equation of wavering, she stepped to Doug's side and, on tiptoe, kissed him full on the mouth. "I admire you, cowboy."

He gathered Jill in his arms and twirled her around, "Jill, I love you, make no mistake on that." He had to sit down. His legs buckled, and he turned pale.

Miss Tally shook her head and spoke, "I made your arrangements, Doug, to Aspen, company billing, and I found Theodor's location. But the winter storm that hit Aspen will make the way touch and go."

"Look at me." He winked and pounded on his chest. "I'm tough. I'll need to go to my tiny house, gather a duffel bag, and stuff it with things."

"I'll leave with you and drive your truck home from the airport." Jill said.

Miss Tally, in verily a whisper, said, "Thanks Doug," she turned to Tara with arm around her said, "We'll be just fine tonight, and since it's so late I'll stay over and sleep in the spare room."

Tara bobbed her head and hugged Miss Tally. She then walked Snow to the back door while sipping her tea, looked upward, and said, "Savior, take care of my uncle and be with Theodor and us if it's not too late."

Miss Tally said, "Amen," and placed her head on Tara's shoulder.

After Jill and Doug were gone, Tara placed another log on the fire, poking it. She went into her room and gave Miss Tally flannel pajamas in which bagged on her, but Miss Tally only smiled and bid Tara goodnight.

The next morning, Miss Tally was dressed and had coffee ready for Tara when she came in the kitchen. She said, "Dear, I'm headed into the office, Jill is picking me up. I've have tons of work to do now that…" Her voice trailed, and a tear fell.

Tara patted her arm and nodded. "I'm on my way in to the animal shelter." She took a sip of much-needed black coffee. "I need to call the veterinary service for a list of available veterinarians to see who can temporary replace Uncle Doug. I don't know how long he'll be out of the country." Rolling her eyes, she continued, "I have rules and regulation given by the state board if I want the clinic to stay open." She let Snow out and waited.

Forty minutes later, Mary Beth met a handsome young male veterinarian. "Hello, my name is Stephen Johns. I'm here for an interview. Is Miss Scott available?"

Mary Beth stared, pinching herself, and said, "Just a minute. I'll phone her office." She stepped away from the desk, asking him to be seated. Third ring. "Tara, hurry downstairs. He's here. Doug's replacement."

Tara ran a brush through her red bouncy hair, glossed her lips, and walked into the waiting office and approached the counter.

Mary Beth, wide-eyed, pointed to the man's back and mouth, and said, "Wow!"

She smiled and approached the young man. "Hello, I'm Tara Scott, and you are Mr. Stephen Johns?"

He stood and was two, maybe three inches taller than Theodor and four, maybe five years younger. Now what brought him to mind? "I am he," he said.

Mary Beth propped her head on her hands at the counter and hung on to every word spoken. After the interview, Tara and Mr. Johns went to her office, signed the necessary paperwork, and shook hands. He said, "Call me Steve, please."

In the foyer, Tara said, "Well, Steve, when can you start?"

"I'm here now. How about a tour in the clinic?"

Her cell phone rang. "Just a minute please." Tara shoved through the clinic's door and motioned to Mary Beth and mouth, "Phone call, show Mr. Johns around." Mary Beth's green eyes were bright.

In her office, she said, "Hello, Miss Tally, any news on Uncle Doug or Theodor?"

"Tsk-tsk. Doug's in Aspen's airport stuck for several hours. More snow fell. But I'm not worried about him. Doug's a man that can take care of himself. It's Theodor I'm concern about. He's at a very low fragile time in his life. I hope Doug reaches him soon."

"Now, Miss Tally, Uncle Doug is reliable and knows how to handle most situations. Snow is in God's timing, however. I'm sure my uncle is aware that time is of essence."

"It just that Theodor is alone."

Tara wanted to say more but settled. "He's a grown man. One who's traveled and stayed around the world. He'll be just fine." The phone lines were ringing at both places, and Tara said, "Thanks for calling. Keep in touch, Miss Tally, and try not to worry. Just pray." Lines silence. And Tara did quickly pray again.

Mary Beth trailed behind Mr. Johns as he stepped into the foyer and said, "I can be back at three today and begin work, Miss Scott."

"Let's use first names, and three is fine." Tara glanced over at Mary Beth and blinked. Was she drooling? Tara smiled and shook his hand. He carried his signed paperwork with him.

Mary Beth said, "What nice eye candy. He's thirty-two. You wouldn't have interest claims on him, would you?"

"Oh, Mary Beth, I'm in a hot mess now for trying to date. He's all yours unless he has a significant other."

Mary Beth bunched her full lips and said, "Well, I'll just ask him!" She caught the ringing phone. "Good midmorning, you've reached Scott's animal shelter, this is Mary Beth speaking." She tapped her long painted nails and said, "Just a moment, I'll check," and pushed the hold button.

Tara was in the clinic only feeding and watering. Her pager went off. Glancing at the caller ID, she answered, "What ya need?"

"There's a frantic woman on the phone wanting to know if we have any Siamese cats. She's considering adoption."

"I have one left, six weeks old, the runt, and she is feisty. Miss Ruby would not be good around young children or dogs. If she's still interested, make her an appointment after three when Steve is here."

"Hello, we do have one cute Siamese kitten left. Her name is Miss Ruby, but she needs lots of attention and should not be around young children or other pets."

"I'm so thrilled. My friend Jill Price thought I could find my delight. My name is Shirley Jones. When can Ruby and I meet?"

"Ms. Jones say four today. We close by five thirty."

"Put me down. Don't let anyone adopt her. Bye." Silence.

Mary Beth set out her packed lunch and insisted that Tara eat. Both ladies hashed over the daily schedule and pushed back to work. Tara went to the back area to leash the dogs and let them run. Time, 2:35 p.m. Mary Beth splashed on perfume and glossed her lips in a bright pink sparkle. She gathered the files and answered calls in a quick manner. Glancing at the clock, it was 2:55 p.m. Steve would soon be at the shelter any minute; her stomach rolled.

"Hello," Steve said in that easy drawl. "Is it Mary Beth?" He smiled.

She nodded; her tongue stuck to the roof of her mouth. She squared her shoulders and willed herself to speak, "Are you on the available market?" Mary Beth covered her mouth. "I'm sorry. That came out all wrong. Not cool."

Steve hardily laughed. "Ms. Mary Beth, you're something else." He walked toward the close doors and paused before entering the clinic. Mary Beth just ended a call; he waited then said, "Were you asking me for yourself? Or a friend?" Eyebrows lifted, and he continued through the doors.

Mary Beth gasped but kept tapping on the computer until Ms. Shirley Jones came in. It was now 4:00 p.m. "Hello." Mary Beth smiled. "Please sign in and be seated. Tara Scott will be right with you."

Only minutes later, a friendly bubblier Tara entered the waiting room. "Ms. Jones, would you like to see sweet baby Ruby?"

She fiddled with her hat pin and scooted her purse up her arm, stood, and said, "Yes, please. I'm so excited. Jill told me to call." Her eyes teared. "My cat of twelve years passed away two weeks ago. My apartment is so silent, no shrill meows. I can't stand it."

Tara nodded and said, "Step this way. Our substitute veterinarian, Steve, has Ruby in the play yard for you to see."

Ruby was leaping and stretching when the three entered the large playroom. Ms. Jones sat down, and, surprisingly in no time, Ruby weaved in and out her legs, meowing loudly. Ms. Jones scratched behind the kitten's ears, and Ruby began purring and still gave her signature loud meow.

"She's marked so beautiful and those light-blue eyes. I'll take her. What shots if any is needed?"

Dr. Steven Johns stated, "Miss Ruby is caught up on everything until next month. You realize the kitten will not ever be a mommy cat?" He smiled.

"I understand."

He handed her the instructions and gave her a copy of the shot record. Next, he gave her soft kitten food and pointed out a collar and leash. Tara walked with Ms. Jones to the counter where Mary Beth rung up the order. She asked, "Do you want to make Miss Ruby's appointment now or call in to schedule for next month?"

"I'll call. I just want to get Miss Ruby home and settled."

Steve carried a heavy-duty cardboard cage with airholes holding a squally Miss Ruby. Mary Beth came around the corner and said, "Let me carry your items, Ms. Jones."

Steve continued out with the package kitten still smiling, lab coat flapping. Ms. Jones opened the front passenger car seat and said, "Oh, Miss Ruby, don't cry. We'll soon be home."

Mary Beth reached in to set her held items on the vehicle's floor as Steve set down the packaged kitten. Their hands touch; Mary Beth eyes opened wider. His were shielded and narrow. Both waved to Ms. Jones and bumped shoulders when they turned. Steve said, "Mary Beth, I'm single. Would you like to have dinner with me after work and perhaps take a walk?"

She smiled, opened her mouth, and breathlessly said, "Yes." Mary Beth hurried and opened the door and rushed to a ringing phone. She glanced up in time to catch his wink. Heat rose from her neck to her pale face, thinking, *This has never happened to me all aggressive woman.*

Tara touched her hand. "You okay?"

"I...I am. Yes, indeed." She reached for the ringing phone again. "Yes, Tara is here." She shoved the phone to her. "It's him. Mr. Dreamy."

Tara's hand shook. "Hello."

"Tara, I'm...I'm, so-r—" The line went dead.

She tapped the line again and again. Nothing. She looked up. "I've lost him. All he said was my name." She bunched her lips and thought, *I wish I had updated our phone equipment, we can't even ID anyone.* She blew out a disgusted sigh.

"He'll call back or Jill or Miss Tally will call you," Mary Beth said.

Nodding, Tara walked through the clinic door and murmured, "I'll call Jill and Miss Tally," when all of a sudden, she heard, "Take a number, take a number, please take a number." It seemed that dogs and cats were in full choir mode. Tara peeked in. Yes, the waiting room was crowded. Tara rushed to the back to warn Steve, "There's going to be a rush on checking in strays no longer wanted for one reason to another." She thought, *People move or the cat/dog has too many offsprings. Well, I'll call the ladies later.* She made quick steps and said, "Steve, answer me. Did you hear?"

"No, what?"

"Prepare yourself. We are flooded with cats and dogs up front." Their pagers sounded; it was Mary Beth.

One by one, Tara and Mary Beth carried animals to Steve, which were placed in different holding pens and closed areas until each animal could be checked all over for general health. Three hours later, well past closing, now 7:00 p.m., the three—Steve, Mary Beth, and Tara—glanced at each other. Steve said, "Good job, ladies." He smiled while washing his hands. "I don't know about you two, but I'm starving. Let's go somewhere and eat."

Tara said, "You two go on ahead. I still have keying input to do."

Mary Beth took Tara's hand and said, "We'll eat then I'll come back and help you with updates." She tugged her arm.

They all got into Steve's yellow spots car and ordered from the McDonald's drive-through. Back at the shop, Mary Beth, Tara, and a helpful Steve entered each animal by name, age, weight, breed, and health status. Now 10:00 p.m. and exhausted, they left the animal shelter.

Tara didn't linger but hurried to catch the last bus. She waved to Mary Beth and Steve who were still in a huddle talking.

Inside her house, Snow butted her thigh and woofed. She reached down and scratched him behind the head and said, "Outside?" Her shy but mysteries newly acquired senior cat, Butter Cup, jumped from the refrigerator and meowed. Tara put feed into the cat's bowl and special blend dog food out for Snow. She watered both and was anxious to call Jill and Miss Tally, wondering if any word had came from Doug about Theodor and to tell them of her mystery call from him. Time, 11:15 p.m., too late to call. Tara dragged into the bathroom, filled the tub to the rim with hot bubbled water, and slid herself in soaked from shoulders down.

# Chapter 12

Doug blew out a held breath. "Miss Tally, hello, I'm made it to the hospital, and Theodor has more than a serious leg breakage. He has a concussion and has suffered memory loss. To what extent, the doctors don't know. However, I need Theodor Welch's updated insurance information and the power of attorney for me to proceed any further. Do you have that authority, Miss Tally?"

"Oh, poor Theodor, tsk-tsk, and, yes, I'll have the insurance information gathered and arrange for the transfer and the signed power of attorney over to you."

"Sorry to cut you off, but I'm being paged. Bye, Miss Tally, keep your chin up."

Miss Tally hurried and called Jill to inform her she had heard from Doug. Two hours later, Jill was at the Columbus airport. Destination: Aspen. She carried Miss Tally's envelope for Doug in hand. Ten hours later, she texted Doug, "Meet me—I'm at Aspen's airport, Jill." She ordered a hot coffee and sat down to wait.

Three hours later, dressed in rugged outdoor wear, Doug greeted Jill first in hug then in kiss and then in hug again. "Jill, what are you doing here? Who's looking after your farm and the Arabian? Oh, it's good to see you." He hugged her tighter.

Jill placed a hand on his chest and stepped back handing him the envelope. "From Miss Tally." She gazed into his blue eyes and said, "Now the farm and stock is under my foreman and his crew. The Arabian will be there when you come back. No one else is to bother him." She kissed him again. "Now, how's the patient?"

"Do you have a place to stay?"

She blushed and shook her head no. "Not yet."

"How long are you here for?"

Jill hunched her shoulders. "Aren't you needed at the hospital since you have the signed paperwork? And don't worry. I'll find a place to stay."

He shoved it into his jean pocket and handed her his flat's key. "Please, Jill, stay at the flat. I shouldn't be too long." He wrote down the address and shoved it into her hand and kissed her hard. He was gone in his long strides.

<hr/>

Jill managed her luggage and arrived at Doug's flat. She was surprised to see the niceness. Although on ground floor, there were two spacious bedrooms. She removed her outer coat and looked around for teabags, coffee, anything hot to drink. She made herself at home and fixed a deli sandwich of cheese and turkey and lied on the sofa.

<hr/>

A gust of wind and snow blew in through the door. Jill bolted upward. *Where am I*, she thought. It was dark inside and out.

Doug whispered, "Jill, are you here?" He switched on a light, and she wrapped her arms around his waist. "Sorry, I doze off a bit."

He smiled. "Thank you for bringing me all the necessary paperwork. Did you get settled in here?"

Her face pinkened. "No. My suitcases are right by the front door, unpacked. I imagined you'd take me to a hotel when you came."

He towered over Jill. "Why not stay here with me. There's plenty of room. There's two bedrooms." He looked down into Jill's brown eyes. "You're safe. No bone jumping. Sorry, men's talk."

She pinkened more. "Alrighty then, I understand, and I know you're a gentleman and a God-fearing cowboy." She went to the sofa and patted the seat. "Tell me about Theodor."

He stepped toward her and said, "Why don't you unpack, and we'll order in tonight and talk over eating."

She stood and he carried her luggage into the spare bedroom and somehow the room no longer seemed so spacious.

"Jill, takeout is here." He pulled out a chair, and she sat down. The fire was lit in the fireplace, and the logs sparked. He updated her with the facts that Theodor had no recollection as to who he was, where he lived, or what he did for a living.

For the next five days, Doug left the flat at daybreak and didn't return until way after dark. On Tuesday evening the following week, Doug crossed his feet after eating and updated Jill on Theodor. "His leg is healing nicely and rehab is to begin soon. I've exalted everything I know to do." His hands flew in the air. "I've showed Theodor pictures, contact names on his cell phone, shown him business cards, and nothing." He shook his head. "His therapist said when the swelling goes down inside his brain, Theodor may remember everything, or not. I'm at my wit's end, Jill."

"Can he travel?"

"How I wish, but no. The doctors all agree that travel at this time would be too dangerous. Even when I'm at the hospital visiting, talking, I don't think Theodor knows me." Doug picked up a cup of hot coffee, sipped, and said, "Tomorrow, Theodor will be in and out of x-rays, physical therapy treatments for the day. I'm on call but not scheduled at the hospital. I was wondering if I might show you around a little village north of here called Holly. It takes you back in time, maybe 1810, and the people are so friendly. Some of the old-timers still remembered me from when I visited here years ago."

"Sure, cowboy, I would love to see the hillside or mountains or ski slopes with you, but are you sure you can spare the time?"

His mouth lifted, and his smile sparkled in his blue, blue eyes.

Jill glanced away to capture just this moment in time. *The heartbreaker Doug must be known throughout the world. He's so authentic, good-looking, and manly.* At that moment, she realized, *I love him, perhaps from the instant I walked into the animal shelter's clinic, and he spoke.* "What were you saying?" Jill asked.

Brow arched, Doug repeated, "I'm sure I'm free, but my time is limited from that point on. I'm sorry, Jill. You've come all this way. I do appreciate you being here. Not only do you cook, clean, and put up with my sober jokes"—he locked eyes with her—"you're fascinating, sensible, and very loveable, Jill." He sighed. "It's only fair to warn you, you've lassoed this cowboy's heart." He stood, kissed her, and their lips lingered.

Jill nervously began tidying up the kitchen, and Doug quickly excused himself and walked in his bedroom with phone in hand. He called Miss Tally as he had every night, giving her latest news, rather any, on Theodor. "What's that, Miss Tally? Will Jill be back in time for the farm's annual Christmas celebration?"

Doug glanced up and saw Jill in the hallway. "Here, Miss Tally wants to know about Christmas."

Without looking his way, she said, "Yes, I've booked my flight out day after tomorrow. I've spoke to my ranch foreman, and the sleighs and horses will be ready for the tours. Bright color lights are on the barn and should be completed within the week. Miss Tally, are you working in the gift store, starting next week?"

"I am. Also Tara, Marry Beth, and the new vet, Steve, volunteered to help with story time and afterward for the children's interacting and petting the miniature horses."

"Tsk-tsk. We need a Santa Clause for our township. Poor Sam twisted his foot and can't wear the big man's black boots. I wish Doug could be here. He's about the same size. Tsk-tsk."

Jill glanced up; Doug's large hands were on his hips.

She spoke into the phone, "Miss Tally, he's staying here with Theodor who truly needs him. We'll think of something. I need to go. His other phone line is beeping." She passed the phone back to Doug and went in her room.

The next morning, Jill made strong coffee. Time was 5:00 a.m. Twenty minutes later, Doug joined her. "You ready for our outing?" He leaned in and kissed her cheek.

She crossed her arms, thinking, *How can any man look so darn good this time in the morning* and blushed. "Yes, let me grab my coat and hat. Oh, here are my gloves." She slipped them on.

"Great coffee this morning!" Doug stretch his coated arms. "Let's head on out."

The rented four-wheel drive SUV kept to the road. A new layer of snow had fallen, and several hours later, both were in Holly. She gasped as she twirled around. Large snowflakes fell. Jill closed her eyes and stuck out her tongue, catching flakes. "It's just like being in a snow globe."

Doug reached for her hand entwining his fingers. Pointing, he said, "To your left are the ski lifts, straight ahead are the zip lines, and over there are the foot trails around the village. What would you like to do?"

Her face was bright and even youthful; she nodded and said, "Zip lining." Breaking her hand free, she clapped and jumped. "I've always thought that would be fun."

He chuckled, and they stepped forward. She yelled and screamed and finally, silence fell, breathing in the beauty of snow-covered assorted pine mountains about the quaint village of Holly. Doug waited at the other end for Jill and helped her get unstrapped.

Reaching for her hand again, they began walking. They hiked well until afternoon. Doug lifted his hand. "Down there is the lodge. We can eat. I'm starving."

"Me too!" Jill thought, *Doug's so confident, manly, and yet tender.*

"We made it." Shucking his feet, he motioned to the left for dinner. Afterward, they walked the village. Children were ice-skating, running, playing tag, or walking with adult caught up in the excitement of shopping. The town tree was decorated and glowed. A group of older men were gathered over an open fire, perhaps conjuring up stories of the past. They waved and continued their yarns. They window-shop, and he asked her to wait as he entered a store. When Doug came out smiling from ear to ear, he presented her with a snow globe containing a couple sky lining. He shook, and the snow fell on the couple as it was on them. He bent and kissed her handing the snow globe.

She pulled him down and returned the kiss and, in a low whisper, breathed, "Doug, I love you." Her face went hot.

He didn't answer but pulled her closer and kissed her hard. She snuggled in more. They had a perfect day, and tomorrow, she would be leaving and going through the hustle bustle of life on the farm and the finality of decorating for the townspeople's enjoyment. Jill closed her eyes for a moment and flashed back in time. As a child, her grandfather decorated and opened the farm with miniature displays, snow people, reindeers, even baby Jesus with Mary and Joseph with real farm animals surrounding the sight, a real traditional Christmas. She could hear her grandfather say, "The horse and sleigh rides helped cover feed cost through the winter."

"Where'd you go?" Doug asked.

"Just thinking of the past and how it's the future still on the farm, the displays, entertainment, and horse with sleigh rides, so much to pull together when I get home."

They finished the day on the ski slope, and Jill felt more confident than ever, only going on the beginner's slope. Doug was good-natured and stayed at her side.

The evening whipped in another storm. With boots off, Doug was reading from Jill's Bible events leading up to the birth of Christ. After prayer, Doug sat forward holding the Bible and said, "Jill, thank you for being a strong person and caring that I know this Savior." He handed her the Bible and stood. "Big world, isn't it?" He glanced out and looked into the starlit sky filled with sparkle. "He's everywhere and yet"—touching his chest—"knocks to come in." He shook his head. His cell phone rang. "Hello, Doug here."

Jill's heart was warm with hope and her love grew more if possible for cowboy. "What's up?"

Stepping into his boots, he said, "The doctor wants to meet with me tonight. Something about an x-ray they took today." He bunched his brow and added, "Jill, I don't know when I'll be back. Take the SUV to the airport. It will get you through the snow." He reached for her again. "You are a piece of heaven." He grabbed his coat and left in a cab.

She was on her own. It was time to pack for her departure in the morning, but she sat for a moment, questioning, "What's life going to be without Doug," and cried. Doug hadn't made any commitment to her except for training Satish the Arabian then he would be gone. "My heart will be broken after all these single years." It was a sleepless night.

Jill unplugged the coffeemaker and rinsed out the pot. She hadn't heard from Doug and didn't know when he would return. She washed and changed the sheets in the spare room and gathered her luggage. It was time to leave. She quickly left him a note, saying, "Thank you for your hospitality and being a true gentleman. I'll miss you, cowboy. Hurry home. Love, Jill." She placed it by the coffeemaker. "Hum, nothing more to say." Jill turned, carried, and pulled her luggage to the SUV.

The roads were treacherous. They were down to one lane, and cars were stranded; some were piled into others. She gripped the wheel. "Come on, girl, this isn't your first rodeo." She paused, thinking of Doug's strength and drew from it. Just then, the SUV slid. Jill quickly turned the wheel and again. She gained control and was glad she was at the airport.

The SUV was parked safely, and she trudged through the foot or more of new fallen snow, dragging her luggage. The airport was crowded with baby crying, people shouting, delays and cancelations posted. Finally, she stepped up to the counter. "Reservations for Jill Price."

Her ticket was rung, stamped, and handed to her. "Miss, hurry, 233 is about to depart. Last one for the day. We're closing down. Next."

She made quick steps, handed over her ticket, and entered the plane. She was relieved to sit down and buckle up. The plane soared; Jill closed her eyes and slept.

⁘⟩ ⁙ ⟨⁘

Tara met Jill at the airport. "It's good to have you home. How's Uncle Doug, Theodor, any updates?" She pulled the luggage to Doug's truck. Snow was falling.

Rubbing her hands together. she said, "Doug has worked endlessly with Theodor and still no results. I'm afraid Theodor's bump on the head has left him without memory. We must pray for a speedy recovery and hope they can return home soon."

"But Theodor called me before you left for Aspen, said my name, and the line went dead."

"I know, child." She touched her cheek. Moments later, Jill said, "How's work and Mary Beth? Do tell me about your new veterinarian."

Tara watched the roads as the snow fell. She answered, "Work has been busy. We had a rush on intake cats and dogs. Steve is wonderful and was quick in examinations and healthcare. Most have been adopted out now, and things are a bit slower. Mary Beth"—Tara giggled—"has a huge case of 'like' on the new vet, Steve. She's moonstruck! And he appears calm, cool, and collect, but he's slyly dating Mary Beth. It's nice to see young love—ahhhh."

"Well, according to Miss Tally, Theodor has a case of something old fashion on you. Well, we're here. Thanks for the ride. Will you be all right driving home or do you want to spend the night?"

"I'm fine. The ride isn't so bad. I'll take my time. See you at the farm tomorrow evening. We've only have a week and a half left to get ready for your amazing Christmas event opening and only four more weeks until December twenty fifth. Ho ho ho."

"See you at six thirty tomorrow evening." Jill forged ahead. It was good to be in her house. The foreman had several list posted to her computer for "Work Event" updates. She unpacked, made a tea, and opened the computer files an hour later. It was now 10:00 p.m. She powered down and took a much-needed shower. Then she slept.

It was now 5:00 a.m. Time to tend to the outside animals and see Jill's foreman. In the barn, she said, "Sam, we need to build a few props. Miss Tally left word she wants the local children to perform a play she's written. Has she been in touch with you?"

He rolled his eyes. "Yes, and I have a few of the men building props and painting scenery. You, on the other hand, will have the community's children to direct."

"Correction, codirect with Miss Tally. There are six practices, and they begin this Saturday afternoon at two thirty."

"We'll be ready. Now when does Mr. Smyth begin training Satish?"

"When he returns with Theodor from Aspen." She sighed. "Right now, it's iffy."

Sam said, "I hear Theodor has a loss of memory among physical problems. How's Miss Tally at her age keeping up with everything?" He whistled.

"She's a cracker all right. We need to keep her in our prayers, strength and all." Jill walked toward the house, kicking her boot at the snow. Inside, she made breakfast, sat down, and pushed her eggs from side to side. She wondered, *Will Theodor be well enough to travel before the new year? And how long can Doug personally stay in Aspen?* Her cell phone rang. Time now was 7:00 a.m. Jill glanced at the ID; it was Doug. "Hello."

"Was afraid I'd have to leave you a message. Glad I caught you. I miss you, Jill." Silence.

"I missed you before I left. What's wrong, Doug? I hear something in your voice."

"Bad round of snow headed in, beside what's already here. I'm staying at the hospital. Transportation became impossible. I don't have my cell charger with me so you won't be able to reach me. The phone lines are down here also. The hospital is on backup generators, the worst storm ever recorded! I left word for Miss Tally on her work's answering machine." He blew out a held breath. "Oh, Theodor said Tara's name this morning when he saw her picture on his phone. Then he fell asleep. Don't know what if anything that means."

"Keep your chin up, cowboy, I lo—" Line buzzed. She tried his number. Dead. Jill dumped her breakfast and called Miss Tally's cell.

"Jill, is that you?" Miss Tally asked.

"Yes, I heard from Doug before the storm hit. He's without phone as is the hospital."

"He left you word at work. Hospital is on generators. And Theodor said Tara's name again."

"I know in his heart Tara Scott is there, and he's reaching out to her and only her. She needs to know! Tsk-tsk."

"You're an old romantic being, Miss Tally." She paced then said, "We do need to talk about this play you've wrote before Saturday. How about dinner Friday evening, say 6:00 p.m.?"

"Fine. I'll see if Tara, Mary Beth, and that new vet, Steve, can make it so we're all on the same page. My cell's beeping. It's Kevin, bye."

# Chapter 13

PLACING HER FORK on the plate, Tara said, "What do you mean Theodor called out to me?" Tara's face paled.

Miss Tally nodded to Jill. "When Doug last called, he said Theodor saw your picture on his cell phone and raised a finger, screeched your name, and then collapsed. None of us understand this, but he's definitely reaching out to you, Tara. You're the only one he seems to recognize."

She blushed. "Why me, a mistake text of who's who? A few dates and nothing." She shook her head. "There wasn't an *us*. As you can see, he left state without word to anyone shortly after our lunch here, Jill. Does that sound like a man who wants commitment or to be in a relationship? Let me answer." Counting one, two, three. "It's a simple no!"

Miss tally came around the table and kissed Tara's cheek and, almost in whisper, said, "He's a proud, confused, stubborn man, but one thing I know"—lifting her wrinkled arm—"is Theodor is battling within himself on stirred-up feelings he has for you, girl."

She gasped, dropping her fork.

Mary Beth stood, made contact with Tara, and said, "Strange way of showing he cares. I wouldn't listen to them, Tara. You put yourself out there for him, and all he's done has been rude and selfish."

Miss Tally said, "Tara, you'll see I'm right, but enough! Let's work on the screenplay. My twin sister thinks the community will love hearing the children sing and say their speaking parts."

Jill cleared the old farm table, and everyone gathered back around. Miss Tally handed Jill the to-do list and said, "Need to add anything to it. Go right ahead."

Jill reached for a pencil, rummaging around the drawer. "Tara, can you make the angle and animal costumes? Check. Mary Beth, will you help out with hair and makeup? Check. Steve, my foreman Sam will need help exchanging out the sleighs and tour guides. Are you up to this cold weather and hard work?"

"I'm from Dakota, and yes, ma'am, add me to the list."

Check. Jill glanced over at Miss Tally. "That's leaves us to find a Santa Clause."

Clucking her tongue, Miss Tally said, "We will. I'll call around."

Sam lightly knocked and entered the kitchen. "Jill, I've moved all the animals to building number 2. The barn will be hosed down and ready tomorrow to build the stage. Then we can begin nailing props and, by the following week, hang curtains with their winter-painted new-and-old-city scenery. There's a lot of work to do." He kept chewing on a straw end.

"How did Satish take the move?" Sam asked.

"He's skittish, moody, powerful, and magnificent all in one. I found out he likes apples. That helped. Doug's going to have his hands full. I'm all eyes when training begins."

Jill handed over work orders to Sam. "Don't you worry about Doug. Some say he's a horse whisperer. My money's on him."

"Heard anything?" Sam opened the kitchen door.

"He's caught in a snowstorm at the hospital and no cell power. Waiting it out." Jill rolled her brown eyes.

Miss Tally said, "Tara, Mary Beth, what do you think of our little play?"

Mary Beth said, "The mixture of songs is good, and they tell a story in itself."

Tara added, "Miss Tally, I think a verse between song number 2 and 4 and maybe 7 is all that is needed." Flipping the papers, she continued, "Well, except for the opening and closing numbers, we can have solos, duets, trios, and groups so no matter how many children attend, they all can be included."

Steve said, "What about refreshments like cookie, hot chocolate, cider, on skit night, before or right after the performance?"

Jill and Miss Tally both sighed in unison. Miss Tally nodded. "We'll get back to you on refreshments. Good call though, Steve."

Mary Beth muttered, "Always looking out for the snacks."

Everyone laughed.

Jill glanced outside. "My, my, the snow has fallen another six inches. I think we've accomplished everything we can tonight."

Steve spoke, "Miss Tally, would you care for a ride into town? I'm dropping off Mary Beth, and I live in the short north just a ways from your area. It'd be no problem, ma'am."

"Sonny, you think we'll be safe in that sporty car you drive? How are the tires?"

Jill muffled a chuckle and so did Tara almost.

❧⟶ ⟵☙

Two week passed. Miss Tally sent Kevin out of town on motivational speaking, and she, with the two clerks, were handling the office. The phones rang off their hooks. Clerk number 1 handled all entries for older clients, clerk number 2 handled all Kevin's client updates, and Miss Tally took care of Theodor's people, including, she said, "If that Elisha or Jeanette or Georgette calls again or stop in this office, I'm going to really tell them off. Tsk-tsk." Shaking her frail fisted hand, she added, "They need to move on. He's taken!"

The clerks looked up, didn't smile, giggle, or laugh; they kept tapping away and answering the busy phone lines.

Two days later, Kevin returned and brought his signed lists of new clients. It was 5:00 a.m., and he still was keying in information. He made a cup of coffee and began again. Fifty new clients were now added, and Miss Tally walked through the door. He quickly grabbed his suit jacket and jabbed his arm in the sleeves. Straightening his tie, he said, "Good morning."

"Kevin, Kevin, you're working like Theodor."

He smiled. "I've never known a man that has his work ethics well or his life. I'm sorry. Have you any news on him? I do trust he'll soon recover and be back."

Miss Tally dabbed at her eyes and just as quickly said, "Kevin, there is more to life than always working and playing hard." She looked over her white-rimmed glasses and pointed that finger. "You, young man, need to find a wholesome God-fearing woman and settle down. Don't you dare get mixed up with the likes of, well"—shaking her hand through the air—"those painted-up hussies." She walked toward her desk and said, "Welcome back, Kevin, and no, there is no word on Theodor. She hung her hat and coat on the rack and proceeded to listen to the answering machine, taking notes.

When number 1 clerk came in, Miss Tally handed her a stack of regular clients wanting information. Number 1 clerk, Terri, said, "Miss Tally, you remember Sherri has the day off?"

Miss Tally bunched her lips. "Tsk-tsk, here is her stack of calls. Better make you a stiff tea or coffee. You'll be a while with the client's calls and inputs." The phone line rang.

"Miss Tally here."

"Good morning, sis. I'm back, and I thought I'd come stay the holidays with you if that's all right."

Miss Tally glanced around the room then said, "I could really use your help with the community project. And yes, by all means come. I love you."

"All right. I can't wait to help out." She paused then said, "I'm coming by Grey Hound bus. Don't worry. I'll take a cab to your apartment from the bus station."

Miss Tally made note: change spare bed linens, add towels to a joining bathroom, call Jill and see where her sister could help with community play. She tapped her nails and went and made a hot tea. Back at her desk the phones were a constant ring.

"Hello, Miss Tally speaking, one moment please hold the line".. The other lines kept ringing off the hook. Again Miss Tally answered, "Hold the line please," and pushed the button on hold. She glanced over to where Kevin was setting, and snipped, "Don't you hear the phones, ringing. Answere them!"

It was midafternoon when Miss Tally called Jill while the others were out to lunch.

"Miss Tally? What's up?" Jill said.

She let out a heavy sigh. "My sister will be here by tomorrow, and I'm afraid I won't be able to spend much time with her as I would like with Theodor, you know, out from the office."

"Oh, Miss Tally, this has to be so hard on you and with all new people in the office. What can I do?"

"How about involving my sister with the music in the play? You know she taught music in school. Don't you need another group meeting? And perhaps she could assist with the sewing of costumes."

"Good idea. I'll call Tara, and she can let Mary Beth and Steve know. How about meeting tomorrow at 6:30 p.m. at the ranch? I'll fix dinner for everyone." Jill made notes as they spoke.

"Jill, I have to go. We're short a worker today. Sherri took a personal day to get her hair highlighted," she said. "I never seen the likes that personal things except for doctor visits couldn't be done after work, tsk-tsk." The phone was ringing again. "See you tomorrow night with my sister, bye."

Another cup of pumpkin-flavored coffee and Miss Tally waved good-bye and added a thank-you to Terri as she left work for the evening. Kevin looked up and said, "Miss Tally, talk about a person over working you need to listen also." He smiled and powered down his computer. "I overheard you say your twin sister is coming for a visit. That will be nice, I'm sure. Just asking, is she anything like you?"

Miss Tally pushed at her white-rimmed glasses. "We're identical in every way except I majored in business and she has a musical degree and three years ago, Meryl retired from teaching to travel. Don't worry, Kevin. I'll be in to work each day." She airlifted her hand. "Now, be off with you, tsk-tsk." Miss Tally took a sip of coffee, breathed in, and continued tap, tapping on the computer's keyboard.

The next evening, Steve picked up both Miss Tallies, and both remarked about his sporty car as they called it. He played classical music low and answered when the ladies included him. Meryl said, "You're a southern charmer."

Miss Cheryl Tally said, "He's originally from Dakota, not the south."

"Well, he must have had a southern parent. Do you, boy?"

He chuckled he was thirty years old and called boy. He replied, "I do have a southern father. Quite the gentleman, I hear. He would have whipped me good if I used slang language or wasn't courteous to my peers."

"Told you," Meryl muttered under her breath in the back seat to her sister.

"Ladies, we're here. Let me assist you, and I want to check if Tara and Mary Beth have arrived. Both Miss Tallies place their arm through his and chattered into the house.

"My, Cheryl, Meryl, so nice to see you," Jill greeted each with a hug and cheek kiss. "Come into the kitchen. Everyone is in there."

Steve seated the sisters and glance Mary Beth's way and winked. She fiddled with her clothed napkin and said, "Miss Tally." Both turned in her direction. "Um, Miss Meryl, I hear you taught music in high school. Jill has a piano. Maybe after dinner you'd play for us."

She threw up her hands, but Miss Cheryl Tally spoke up, "She'd love to play. After all, she is a concert artist." She smiled and patted her sister's hand.

The meal was served, prayer was given, and after way too much food and apple pie desert, no one could think of working on the community play. Miss Meryl Tally rose and sought the piano. Everyone gathered in the huge living room. Meryl lifted the covering and slid her fingers down the ivory. She scooted out the bench and placed herself erect and played Bach movie theme songs "Fiddler on the Roof" and "Casablanca." She added ragtime, making the ivory keys bounce; then she slowed things down, playing holiday music. "Sing, everybody."

Everyone joined in and clapped when Meryl lowered the piano covering. "Thanks. That was fun. Now what about the upcoming community play?"

Tara said, "I need help with materials and in making angels and animal costumes."

Jill walked over to the hallway and darted out of sight. Shortly, she returned with a basket of material. "Tara, I've collected materials for years to make quilts, but as you see, I have materials. Can you use any?"

Both Miss Tallies rummaged through the basket holding up one piece of material at a time. "Tara, this will do, and this, and how about this." Said the office Miss Tally.

Tara giggled and nodded. She looked over at Jill. "Maybe if it's not too much trouble, we should sew the costumes over here. What do you think?"

All three pair of eyes were on Jill. She placed her hands on her plumped hips and said, "As long as you don't figure me in on the sewing, my place is fine."

The Tallies gathered around each side of Tara and material selections were made. Steve helped Mary Beth with dishes. He washed, she dried, after whispering to him, "Just did my nails."

He took her hand afterward and said, "And they are lovely, and your hands are so soft." His full lips uplifted, and his hazel eyes twinkled. She blushed.

The house phone rang. Jill looked around. No one seemed to notice. She stepped into the pantry. "Doug, my goodness. It's good to hear from you."

"I've missed you too." He cleared his voice. "Update on Theodor. His leg is mending well. Matter of fact, he is walking. Of course, limited and with brace. His memory has accepted me, and he mentions Tara, but rambles. His words make no sense. But we nodded and encouraged him to go on. The doctors feel Theodor can return to the States, but under strict supervision. Not so much with nurses or such, and they say he should not recover at his house. Far too public."

"I have an idea." She let out a held breath. "I want to tell you Miss Tally's twin sister is here. They are identical, oh yea." She snickered. "Now, Cheryl has been working way too many hours and is grieved with not being able to see Theodor. His business would be up a creek without her."

"Jill, darling, where can Theodor stay? We are heading your way next week. The doctors are transferring his records to Doctor's West Hospital. I thought central for all concern in his travel."

"Are the airlines open?"

He could feel her smiling. "Yes, some flights are available. However, Theodor must have a straight flight so, Jill, listen, there's no other way." He blew out a breath. "The man Theodor was visiting has his own plane service, and we'll be aboard his jet."

In a whisper, Jill asked, "Is that woman with you all?"

"Yep! Her father is also taking her back to Ohio. She's not into Theodor and certainly not me, as I am not into her, just so you understand." He sighed. "Jill, you're all the woman I want! The doctor's coming. I've got to go. However, Georgette met one of Theodor's doctors, and they are an item. I mean engage. She's only coming back to gather her clothes, car, and close out her apartment. I don't know if it is love, but most highly *like* I've ever witness." Silence.

Jill hung on the receiver and willed down her joy. Then she realized Theodor needed a place to stay. "Miss Tally, Cheryl, we need to talk."

❖

"Oh, he's coming home." Cheryl clapped her shriveled hands. "Now where can he stay?" She glanced around the room. "Jill"— with laughter in her voice—"since my sister is here for the holidays, she can do most of the sewing, and she knows the music, so why not have Mary Beth a little more involved with the play, and Tara can care for Theodor." She nodded her head, adding, "She has the room. And Steve possibly can keep on working at the shelter, and Doug can help Steve out when he's not at your place. Working, that is."

Jill sat down, wondering, *Did Miss Tally's mind ever unwind.*

"Well, what do you think, Jill?" Cheryl asked.

"Let's call your sister in here first and get her thoughts on if she's willing to take on more and help out."

Miss Tally walked into the other room, and, after seeing Tara was busy pinning different names and sizes to the material, she tapped her sister's shoulder and motioned her to shush. "Follow me."

In the kitchen, Jill explained the program situation and the sewing project's needs to Meryl. The other Miss Tally nodded her head. Meryl tapped her fingers on the table and said, "Might I have another tiny sliver of apple pie?"

Jill scurried and placed a piece of warm apple pie and fork at Meryl's setting. "Enjoy."

Both Jill and Cheryl stared at Meryl, waiting for an answer. Finally, after wiping her mouth, she said, "Of course I'll help. Glad too. And this poor Mr. Welch"—she bunched her lips— "no, no, he needs our encouragement and Tara's help. I agree with Cheryl. That man is smitten with Tara, but she's not at all inclined to think so."

Miss Tally clucked, "Tsk-tsk. Love will win over, just wait and see. But now we need to ask permission for Theodor to stay at her house. Oh my, and what about Doug's thought on the matter?"

Jill blushed. "Let me handle cowboy. And why not wait until Theodor is here before saying anything to Tara? You never know if anything will change between now and then."

Both Tallies giggled. After Jill cleared the kitchen table and made tea, she joined the sisters, Tara, Mary Beth, and Steve. Jill asked, "Anyone for a cup of piping hot tea?"

# Chapter 14

Doug called Miss Tally late Tuesday evening and updated her on Theodor's progress and to expect them in on Wednesday afternoon at 1:15 p.m. Jill had arrived in Doug's SUV at the Columbus airport and parked in a handicap lane. She heard, "Move it, lady, you can't park there."

She slapped a handicap sign on the rearview mirror and stuck her tongue out, quickly covering her mouth and thinking, *Not very Christian-like.* She said, "I can, and I have." Jill mused, *I'm glad Miss Tally borrowed the handicap sign from old injured Santa Clause man.* She unbuckled from her seatbelt and opened the back SUV's door, climbing in place the backseat in almost a lying position for Theodor. She waited.

Doug wheeled Theodor outside the airport and lifted him as though he were a sack of potatoes. Theodor's features were solemn and his eyelids kept fluttering. After he was strapped in the seat, Doug folded the wheelchair and placed it in the SUV. He walked Jill around to the passenger side, opened the door, bent down, and kissed her. Raising his head, he said, "Mmm, I've missed you." He kissed her lightly again. "Where to, gorgeous?"

She patted his gloved hand and smiled. "He'll be staying at Tara Scott's place." She put a finger to his partly open mouth. "With the holiday play and costumes in the making and the children's practices, Miss Tally and I thought, oh, and her sister,

Meryl, that Tara is the only one who can care for him. After all, she cares for injured animals." Hands floating in the air, she leaned in and kissed him.

"Well, I'm not sure. I like those arrangements!"

"Doug, you know you'll be tied up with Steve at the shelter and in your spare time with my Arabian. The fillies need breed, and according to Sam, Satish is still skittish, but Sam found out he likes apples. I know your time is limited, my wonderful man. And Miss Tally is covering at the office for Theodor and then her sister is here for the holidays. Mary Beth is doing an excellent job at the shelter, and, in the evenings, she meets with me and Meryl four times a week to sew. Steve is working with Sam, and his men are mapping out the grounds for the tours and getting the sleighs ready for the horses to pull."

"Well—" Horns were honking.

Jill grabbed the handicap sign and stuffed it in her purse. "Just drive, Doug, it will be all right." She glanced in the back at Theodor. "Besides, what could possibly happen? The poor man." She sat back in her seat, clutching her purse.

Doug parked in Tara's driveway. "Is she home?"

"Not yet. Let's get Theodor settled in the spare room, and I'll call the shelter for Tara." She smiled. Jill reached for the house key under the artificial pot of flowers that Miss Tally informed her where to look and opened the door. Snow rushed woofing, but Jill grabbed his collar. "Doug, should I put coffee on?" She switched on lights and opened the back door for Snow. She checked the food pantry and was pleased it was stock. She reached into the refrigerator and saw Miss Tally had prepared several dinners and all they needed were to be heated. She removed one and set the oven to preheat.

Doug came in the kitchen and poured a coffee then spoke, "Jill, I'll stop by the clinic and meet Steve what's-his-name, check things out, then I'll bring Tara home. Will you be okay alone with our patient?"

"Sure, and I'll hitch a ride with you when you return. I'm sure you're anxious to see Satish. And I'm excited for you to work with him" She smiled.

Doug nodded, sipped the coffee, then pulled Jill on his lap. He nuzzled her neck and dropped gentle kisses. His breathing became rushed. He lifted his head and said, "Jill, I—"

She stroked his face and ran her hands through his red-brown wavy hair. She pulled his long hair at the nape and whispered, "I love you too." They kissed.

He lifted Jill to her feet, and he followed. "Better let Snow in, and I need to leave." He shifted his Stetson and jingled the keys. At the doorway, he said, "Woman." Shaking his head, he closed the door, and she heard the SUV roar off.

Jill dialed the shelter. "Hello, Mary Beth, please get Tara on the phone now."

"Jill, this is Tara."

"Listen to me. Your uncle is on his way to meet Steve and check out how thing are. He'll also be bringing you back home."

"Is Theodor back?"

"I'm getting to that." She paused and blew out a held breath and quickly inhaled. "Doug brought Theodor home by special flight, and he is in your spare bedroom. We've elected you as his caregiver for now. Sorry, I've got to go. The oven bell dinged. Your dinner will be ready for you both when you arrive."

Jill's hands were trembling. She poured herself a coffee and blew then sipped it down. She checked on Theodor, and he was sleeping as she expected. Jill hurried and made a pitcher with ice water for Theodor's bedside and wrote down his care instructions, hospital number should there be needed, and prayed Tara would comply and not complain. Then she called Miss Tally for update.

Tara rushed in the door, and Snow greeted her. She scratched his head and said, "Jill?"

A hand was thrown in the air, and she motioned. "On phone." The oven dinged. "Get that." And Jill walked toward the front door, nodding.

Doug hunched his shoulders, calling out, "See you later, Tara." The door shut.

Tara made it to the front door just in time to peek out and see the SUV's taillights fade. She had questions and no answers. She was angry, but why? She heard a frail voice, "Tara?"

Her hand flew to her chest. "It's Theodor." Tara rounded the corner with Snow, and the rugged man she knew was now frail, thinner, paler, and helpless with a slight smile and was shirtless in pajama bottoms only.

He reached out his shaky hand and said, "Home," and passed out.

*What am I going to do?* she thought. "Snow stay." She went into the kitchen and made a food tray and saw medicine by the note on the table. She slipped the medicines on the napkin and went into her new patient's room. Setting the tray on the nightstand, she said cheerily, "Well, hello there. Let me put some pillows behind you and prop you up some. Can you scoot?"

He smiled. Theodor was dead weight. She sighed and climbed on the bed and placed her hands under his arms and lifted and tugged him upward. Her bright-red locks fell forward. He slid a finger around a curl.

"Say, it's nice to have you back and sorry you suffered a terrible fall. After you eat, I'll take a look at your leg." She reached to untangle her hair from his finger and realized she was close to his face. Just a slight movement and they'd kiss. Tara thought, *He's helpless*, and jumped from the bed.

She brought the tray to the bedside and saw he wasn't lifting the fork or picking up any food. Tara bowed her head and prayed, "Lord, heal Theodor and give me strength and wisdom. Also thanks for the food." She shifted the plate and scooped a bite of chicken casserole on the fork. "Open your mouth, Theodor, that's good." She waited and repeated the same order over and over.

An hour later, Theodor pointed toward his crutches. He said, "Bathroom."

She was surprised and glad he said anything; however, working with his weight and to angle him to the commode was another thing.

Theodor in a raspy voice said, "Go."

She paced from the room.

He croaked, "Tara."

She braved a smile and said, "I need to gather a few things for your sponge bath. Stay." She worked quickly and gathered a top-and-bottom pajama, toothbrush, comb, shaver, and said, "I've got everything." Her hands were shaking. Tara filled the sink with warm water and suds up the washrag. She began with his right arm and moved to his solid chest and swirled the washrag around, trailing the curled hair to his pajama band. She was blushing. She moved her hand to rinse the washrag and proceeded the same path on his other shoulder, only inhaling soap and him.

His eyes followed her; no words were uttered. She finished the left arm, side, and slid to the back where she breathed again. The top chore was over and shirt top on and buttoned. He lifted an eyebrow and carefully stood holding on to the sink. She shook her head. "No, no, the bottom is all you." She reddened and suds the cloth. She handed it to him and quickly left the room. She heard a weak chuckle. That was good. She smiled.

He waved off shaving, and his shoulders began to slump. Theodor was so weak. She brought in the wheelchair, brushed his teeth, and combed his thick black hair, and said, "All right, Theodor, are you ready for bed?"

He touched her arm and an electric current sizzled through her body to her toes.

She glanced at him, but he was patting the bed. Tara helped him into bed and placed the covers up midway. She turned on the TV and switched the channel to sports. Tara moved his hair, which flipped forward, off his forehead, and her fingers lingered.

He dozed. She thought, *This assignment is going to be touchy, but he needs me.* She glanced at his face again; his facial muscles were relaxed. Tara made a fire in the fireplace, changed into sweatpants and shirt, made up the couch for it was closer to the spare bedroom, Tara lied on the sofa and pulled the blanket over her. The TV was low. She woke to Snow tugging on her sleeve and heard, "Tara."

She rushed in the room to find Theodor sitting in the wheelchair. She gasped.

"Shame, you should have waited on me." Then she smiled. "Want coffee?"

He smiled and said, "Yes."

Tara nodded. "But you should be in bed fast asleep. It's three in the morning." She moved quickly in the kitchen, and the fresh pot was brewing. Seconds later, she carried a black mug of piping hot coffee to him. He looked at the cup and then at her. Tara left the room only to return with a spoon. "Here, blow, then taste, Theodor." She showed him over and over until he tried. The cup was mostly empty. She blotted his mouth then said, "Let's get you to bed."

He managed to stand. Tara removed the pillows and aided him to lie down. "Raise your head." But she lifted him and stuck two pillows under his head. He slept.

Tara woke from sleep and poured old coffee and added two sugars and two dabs of cream. She placed the mug in the microwave for sixty seconds and at the sound of a beep, she sat down, closed her eyes, and surprisingly enjoyed the taste. She needed to make out a daily schedule for Theodor and think of him as a helpless patient and not the assured man she had danced with. *Would he ever be back?* She let Snow out for a quick jaunt.

Tara heard a light tap on the front door. It was daylight and cold. "Hello, Uncle Doug, your in time for coffee?" She poured a cup.

Doug poked his head into the other room and saw a sleeping Theodor. Sitting down, he said, "How'd last night go?"

"No lie. It was different, but I'm glad I can help."

He sipped his coffee. "Tara, it's real nice of you to care for him. Theodor only has Miss Tally and you know she's older and her sister is in town. Boy, she's something else too." He chuckled.

"Theodor is making progress. He spoke a few words and stood twice around me, which wore him out. He's so weak. His fall was worse than we knew." Tara shook her head. "And what about his doctor visits? I don't have a car."

Nodding, Doug said, "I'm his chauffeur, you're his caregiver, and I'll need for you to go with us." He pulled from his coat pocket written dates for Theodor's neurological and surgeon appointments and the times for him to see his bone specialist.

"Tara."

She rose.

Doug lifted a hand and glanced her way. "I've got this. Go shower and change your clothes."

She obeyed, dressed, and went into the kitchen. She sniffed at the aroma that wavered under her nose and her stomach growled. She touched his shoulder. "Hi, Theodor."

A smile graced the left side of his mouth. Doug placed a spoon in Theodor's hand and encouraged him to eat. "Tara fix you a plate."

Tara savored every mouthful of eggs, sausage, and fried potatoes and dipped the buttered toast in her coffee. "I was hungry. Thanks, Uncle Doug."

"Welcome, but breakfast is your main meal." He turned his head a little and said, "You made a smart move hiring Steve. He's kind to the animals and has a good head on his shoulders, and what a worker."

"I know. How are Mary Beth and he getting along? Did you pick up on them?"

Doug chuckled. "Ah, young love." He caught Theodor grinning. Doug continued, "That female beagle dog had a litter of pups this morning, four yelpers." He hand over hand lifted another bite to Theodor's mouth. He glanced at Tara. "I have a date in an hour with Satish the Arabian stallion, long day today." He smiled. "Tara, take over for me."

Thirty minutes later, Theodor was getting his sponge bath. He reached a hand to Tara's face. "You are pretty." His hand dropped. The light touch and heat from his fingers stayed.

Tara cleared her throat. "Thank you." She helped him into bed and said, "You better hurry and get well, Theodor. All those sophisticated worldly woman are waiting for you." She tucked the covers around him. "And questions have rumored where is bachelor Theodor. I hope you know you're safe here, but then my life is quite calm and not at all glittery." Snow lied on the floor. She glanced up, and Theodor was asleep.

The next few evenings and days rolled into one, until two and a half weeks passed.

With the holiday season upon them, Tara hadn't seen her work friends or much of her uncle Doug. She read e-mail updates from Steve and Mary Beth concerning the shelter and the animals. Miss Tally—Cheryl—called twice, informing her on the holiday event coming up, and bragged rightfully so on her sister's music abilities. Jill had brought over several homemade meals and apple pie though the visits were short. Jill made no mention of the farm or her stallion. On her last visit, Jill received a call stating the north fence was down and she had to leave and gear up for the trail.

Second week in, Theodor was able to shower and feed himself and hold a civil conversation. The following week, the doctors released him from personal care with a good bill of health of the leg and in his concussion. Tara was both happy and sad. Now three days before Christmas Eve, Theodor handed her a wrapped gift and said, "Tara, thank you for being a text kind of person and opening your door to me in a time of need." He stood easily and walked behind her, breathing on her neck.

"What are you doing?" She fluffed her hands.

The corners of Theodor's lips uplifted. "You don't know?" He turned her to face him holding her arms. "Tara, you're a fine woman, kind, one in a million, and passionate about life. What I'm saying is, I can't picture my life without you."

She twisted away, still holding the wrapped package. "Theodor, you're just feeling grateful and overwhelmed because we've bonded through this incident. Now that you're well enough to live at your townhouse and go in to work, well, life will be fun and enjoyable for you again. Here." She reached out her hand to his. "I'm sure these are invitations to parties from now through New Year!" She looked at the gift and placed it under her little artificial Christmas tree setting on an end table. "I'll open it on Christmas. Thanks for the thought. Come on, Snow, outside."

The doorbell dinged. Theodor called out, "Tara." The doorbell dinged again. He opened the front door. "Doug, thanks for picking me up." He glanced at his packed bag. "You've been and 'ace in the sleeve' kind of man, I wouldn't be alive without you. *Thanks* is such a small word." He clapped Doug on the shoulder.

Clearing his throat, Doug said, "Ready then?" Doug momentary looked around, picked up Theodor's tote bag, and thundered, "We're leaving."

Tara was on her cell phone and waved. The door closed, and Tara hung up the phone. She went into the spare room and stripped the bedding; Theodor's manly smell still lingered. Tears threatened. Why was she sad? Theodor had been a perfect gentleman. She sighed, realizing he didn't need her anymore. She showered, tossed the bedding in the washer, pulled her hair into a messy bun, and shoved into her boots and coat and said, "Guard the place, Snow." She went to the bus stop and waited on her ride to the shelter, shaking her arms. "Finally, things will be back to normal."

Mary Beth rushed to hug Tara. "We've missed you. Steve's in the back giving the beagle puppies their first worming and shots." She stared at her. "Well, what about you and Mr. Dreamy?" She was all smiles.

With hunched shoulders, Tara said, "He left. The doctor gave him thumbs up, and I'm here. Now no more talk about Theodor. Don't even mention his name. It was nice to be a temporary 'Florence Nightingale,' but animals are the loving ones." She walked into the clinic.

Steve looked up, and a smile was on his face. "Nice to see you are back?"

Tara softly answered, "Yes, where's those cute puppies I heard about."

They walked to the back and in a closed-off area, she knelt and reached for the brown, black, and white long-eared pup. "Aren't you the cute one." She nuzzled her nose to his face. The others seemed happy to dance around her body and yelp.

# Chapter 15

Doug had just left the animal shelter and rushed over to meet with Jill in hopes of them hashing out the work terms for the Arabian. However, when he entered the mudroom of the kitchen, she was bustling around, in apron, fixing the dinner meal. She said, "Howdy, cowboy, I'm trying to get ready for the two Miss Tallies, Tara, Mary Beth, and Steve. It's our final evening of fitting the children in their costumes and making decisions on their makeup and hairstyles." She glanced up. "There's a costume hanging in my room I need you to wear on Christmas Eve."

He leaned in and brushed her full lips lightly. The car doors were slammed. "Looks like the group had arrived." With hands in the air, Doug said, "What do you need me to do, Jill?"

She bunched her lips then said, "Put another place setting out, yours." She stirred the buttered potatoes and clicked off the oven, catching his eye. "Sam needs another trailblazer with the sleigh one that goes ho ho ho for the holidays. We've rather tied him up in moving the program's props throughout the scenes and the curtains. Are you interested?"

"I can surely help out, but what about Satish?"

She sighed. "Can you see I'm at wit's end." She blew out a held breath. Finally, the doorbell rang. "I'm sorry." She placed a hand on his arm. "Let's table the 'talk work' about the stallion until after the holidays?" She searched his blue eyes.

Nodding slightly with a lazy smile, Doug opened the door. "Hello, everyone." His smile widened. The women were all buzzing, and the Tallies were holding tightly on to Steve's arms.

Jill hollered, "I'm in the kitchen."

They all gathered around the long rustic table and held hands. Doug prayed then country-style passing of the food began. There was laughter, words flowing, and still they ate. And just as quickly as they set down, each rushed out of the house to the barn leaving the dishes set. At Jill's request, she lingered. Doug thundered, "Steve, wait up. I need a crash course on where the trail route begins and end or rather Santa Clause does."

Steve waved. "Come on. I'm headed to the back horse barn to hitch the workhorses." Glancing over his shoulder, he added, "We can do a double team tonight. The snow seems just right for the sleighs."

Doug pulled the coat collar up, tucked down his hat, and said, "A ride over the trails will make a more confident us. Let's giddyup."

Four days passed and Christmas Eve was upon them. Jill's heated barn was beautifully arranged with seating to hold the local community, and outside, the rented covered wagons stood with the farm help ready to serve free food and hot chocolate to the locals. Doug dressed as Santa Clause and Steve as one of the elf with horses and sleighs were on standby.

Seventy children ran in the building from the ages of five through twelve to quickly bestow their costumes, baby lambs, adult sheep, cows, donkeys, chickens, and yard dogs, along with one preteen Joseph, Mary, and a rushed-in wheeled baby portraying little Jesus. The paint curtains were hung, and the prop scenery, trees, bushes, stable, manger, straw, and makeshift fence were in place.

The audience filtered in, and the lights were lowered then uplifted. A request was made for all to be seated. Tara raised her hands, stepping up to the mike in front of the now dropped curtain, and said, "We"—opening her arms wide—"welcome you tonight to the Annual Community Program. Hosted by Jill Price."

Clapping and howling continued. Suddenly, a wolf whistle was heard, and all eyes were on Doug as Santa Clause. He said, "Ho ho ho! Let the little lady speak and then cheer." He disappeared through an open slit curtain.

Tara smiled. "I'll introduce our program's staff then the play will begin. Over at the piano to your left"—arm extended—"Is Meryl Tally, a concert musician in from New York City, and to the right of her is twin sister, local lady, Miss Cheryl Tally, author of the play and administrator to Edwin Jay's Investment Company located at Main and High Street in Columbus, Ohio. She also aided in making our children's costumes." She waited for the applause to quiet down again. "Next to me is Mary Beth Sil, receptionist from Scott's Animal Shelter, and Jill Price, our city's known horse breeder and cattle rancher. Both ladies are the ones in charge of makeup and the children's hair fashion." Another round of applause came. She waited then said, "Sam, stepped out from behind the curtain."

He motioned and, quietly shaking his head, said, "No need to introduce me."

Tara smile radiantly. "Folks, without Sam's knowledge in wood crafting, there would be no stage or props."

The audience whistled, clapped, and stilled as the lights lowered. Tara tapped into the mike. "After the close of tonight's program, Santa Clause's helper, my uncle Doug Symth, known as world bronco star/veterinarian, and Elf, Steve Johns, our town's veterinarian at Scott's Animal Clinic, will be available in hosting the sleigh rides." She stepped through the curtain and a painted outdoor scene of evergreen trees surrounded the children, which opened in a group song entitled "I Wish You a Merry Christmas."

The curtain changed to an old-age village backdrop then the wonderful familiar Bible story began. Joseph paced and finally stood behind a young Mary. She was touching the baby wrapped in like swaddling cloth, lying in the manger. A quartet of children off to the side sang "Away in the Manger." Then at the other side, another quartet group sang, "Angles We Have Heard on High."

The barn door opened, and children entered dressed as sheep and shepherd's costumes, walking slowly forward toward the stage and kneeling in front of the baby. The piano trilled and increased with sound. Older children in camel costumes walked beside the dressed wise men. As the piano sound clip-clop, they knelt before the child. The piano began softly playing and some children sang "It Came Upon a Midnight Clear." Miss Cheryl Tally flapped her hands leading the children on. Then the gold, myrrh, and Frankincense, make-believe gifts, were presented. The wise men said, "To the king!"

Sam unnoticeably changed the painted curtain background, showing a heavenly host of stars in the sky and a huge bright-yellow star stationed over the stable. There was a moment of quiet. Then Tara motioned to Jill, Mary Beth, and down to the Tallies, along with all children standing, and they sang "Silent Night."

Tara shifted and said, "Mary Beth, Jill, please lead the children from the stage to the changing area and then to join their assigned adults." She spoke into the mike, "Thanks, everyone, for coming out, and we trust you enjoy your evening. Happy holidays and be safe. Remember, food, drink, and sleigh rides are available. Oh, is that Santa's bells?"

Clapping and hooting and cheering with men's hats thrown in the air continued until no one was left on stage. Tara stepped down and ran her fingers over the closed piano and glanced around the now almost empty barn. She gasped. Theodor Welch stepped forward. "Tara, wait!"

She grasped her hands.

"I want to thank you for the plug to my business and what a great program, a true gift from all of you and the children of the community. I was blessed," he said.

"Um, you're welcome." She turned to leave, a bit shaken.

"Tara." A hand rested on her cheek. "I'm here also to ask you out for New Year's Eve on a real date."

She shook her head no, but he tilted her chin up. "Tara, I'm serious, I'm not seeing anyone else nor do I want to. My feelings run deep about you." Theodor locked eyes with her. "While I was on the ski slope before the accident, I realized my fear, and it was commitment to a woman, the ball, and chain. But you're not the run-of-the-mill woman, nothing like I've ever associated with all my life. Those women were only out to make a name for them or were interested in me for my money or fame. Tara, please." He blew out a staggering breath. "My love." His bright steel eyes darkened on her wide sky-blue eyes. "I'm in love with you, and I want to court you and see if you find any sincere lasting feelings toward me." He pulled her closer to him. "Am I making a fool out of me?"

Doug walked into the barn unannounced looking for Tara. He walked to her side and said, "Give the poor man a chance," and chuckled. "Santa wants to know if you are ready for the last sleigh ride of the season? Here's your hot chocolate." He smiled and slapped Theodor on the back.

At eleven that night, Jill walked around the outer barn, waiting on Doug to come back. He had taken Tara home. The Tallies, Mary Beth, Steve, and Theodor were long gone. Jill shook her head and said, "That Miss Tally knows everything. I can't believe she just called me, saying Theodor asked Tara out on a promising date to his New Year's company dance." She noticed the truck's headlights appearing as the truck came up the lane. She smiled. "It's cowboy."

Doug walked in with Jill to the barn and stacked chairs for the rental company's pickup. Then with a kiss, he reached for her hand and said praises to Jill for the program and the farm's delightful festivity. They closed the barn's door, and under the outside decorated overhead lights, Doug paused and dropped to one knee.

"Jill." As he reached for her left hand, he cleared his throat and said, "You make my body weak yet strong. I can't imagine a woman of your strength, beauty, or faithfulness ever find the likes of me interesting or husband material, but..." He looked up into Jill's brown eyes and said, "I've loved you from the first time you came into the animal clinic with Butch, and it's only been you ever in my life, others were just likes." He squeezed her hand. "Jill, will you marry me? And soon?"

She felt heat travel from her neck to her face. "Get up, you old coot!" She jerked on his arm. "Okay, we'll get hitched."

He still didn't move.

"Doug, I'm scared. I've never let a man in. I do love you, and my answer is yes."

He let out a held breath and a yee-haw, rose, and not losing contact with Jill. He reached into his sheep skin jacket pocket and pulled out a red velvet box. She jumped up and down her boots, splattering him. He flipped the lid open. She gasped loudly. "Oh, Cowboy." Tears were flowing.

He pulled the yellow-gold one carrot solitaire round diamond from the box and slid it on her left hand ring finger. "My love, do you need space?" he asked. When she just stared and didn't speak, he shuffled from one foot to another then kissed her soundly before swinging her around.

⟶⟩•⟨⟵

Two weeks later, with the assistance of Miss Tally and Tara, Doug and Jill were married in the little church chapel on Broadway.

They went to dinner at IHOP of all places. Jill didn't care; she'd gotten her cowboy. They agreed to postpone their honeymoon until the following year when the Arabian mares were bred. Love was shown all around them as Jill clung to his arm. He nestled her near and gave her kisses, kisses, and more kisses.

They didn't sign any prenuptials for they established everything acquired or would be obtained belonged to each other. Jill was a rich woman, a given free deeded farm containing healthy beef cattle and a lifetime of showing and breeding horses. Doug was equally wealthy, Jill found out. He had most all his bronco winnings and monies that he invested while working from farm to farm, cow punching and horse whispering.

Doug settled on the farm and life began at 5:00 a.m. each day and their home was warm and fussy. He led with devotions and then Jill would talk with Sam and head out when needed with the cattle, or the field fencing, or mucking out the stalls. Sometimes she would ride over to the tiny house and stopped in and have coffee with Sam's wife.

Doug would head to the heated barn and work religiously with Satish. It was the later part of winter and a balmy twenty degrees. On this mutinously day, he wiped his forehead with a bandana and whispered, "Satish Adhem." The horse moved his ears as if waiting for the rest of Doug's wise words or praise. Doug slowly eased and said, "It's only a halter, easy boy." A pat across the horse's neck and some slice apple and the halter was on and soon adjusted. Satish snorted, but Doug continued in his whispered voice of praise, and Satish settled and nuzzled him. Day by day, Doug carefully added the lead and began the long road in training the strong-minded stallion in stop-and-go demands, practicing the art of performance. But his work didn't end with Satish; Doug was in charge of the other farm's fillies and stallion in their breeding program. Sometime his days and evenings rolled into one.

Six months quickly passed, and the prancing Satish Adhem was a magnificent sight to see and watch. Doug worked wonders with the seven-year-old stallion. The time came to introduce a blanket and the saddle he purchased. At first, Satish pawed with his hoof and wildly bucked. Doug was persistent, but kind and calm. "All right, let's try the saddle again only with me on it." He put his boot tip in the strip and swung over the horse's back. Doug quickly wrapped his left hand around the reins, attaching to the saddle horn and in the air went his right hand. His chaps were flapping as the stallion bucked, kicked, and hopped, then sidestepped, and reared. Doug was thrown. This went on until one magical day when Doug spoke softly, "Settle down, big boy." The dust rose, nostrils flared. Satish hoofed at the ground then repeatedly reared. He bucked, and the action grew, but Doug stayed on the horse's back until the stallion surrendered and spiritedly walked. Doug whispered into the ears of the horse and was able, after a standstill, to slide from Satish. He abruptly use the lead commands to stop and go. Afterward, he walked the stallion, wash, rinse, and gave him a complete rubdown and offered him apples.

In the evening at dusk, the sky shared its brilliant colors of rose, purple, and gold lines. Doug would dust off his chaps and wipe his boots before entering the kitchen through the mudroom. "Say, Jill, my mouth is watering."

She'd laughed and playfully said, "Wash up, cowboy, and sit down. The stew will soon be served."

The time came to introduce Satish to the Spanish fillies. Doug patted the stallion's neck and rewarded the stud with several apples. The tall stallion successfully bred all five fillies within a course of one month. The Arabian became calmer. Doug enjoyed the peace and tranquility with the awesome spirited horse and said to his ears, in which tipped inward, "You're beautiful. So powerful, and your foals will be awesome, not to say priceless."

Some days Doug would saddle up Satish and he loved it when the winds were at his back.

In the evening, either Jill or Doug would cook. Life was blissful. A stroll in the moonlight was welcome, or on occasion, having a few friends over for a night of bridge, but Doug always ended his day with an arm over Jill's waist and to the feel of her cold feet in the bed. Doug wondered how had someone not snapped up his beautiful Jill before. Was he ever a lucky man.

Jill enjoyed the rounds out with Sam, and on this particular day, she helped patched the north fence. She waited for the final stretch of wire to be anchored before pounding in the nails.

Sam asked, "How you all doing?"

She smiled and removed her rawhide glove, wiping her forehead, squinting, and saying, "Sam, he's my yang to my ying. I'm so happy, really contentedly happy." She busted out laughing. "Sam, he's warm, kind, loving, and boy does he know horses. According to Doug's records, Satish foals should birth late December into January 2017. I hope I can part with them."

"Yes, Doug's a good man. And, ah, Jill, you're a born businesswoman. Think of what each foal will be worth."

As she was mounting her horse, Jill stretched her eyes, looking across the acreage. "Sam, my grandfather sure had a vision not just in cattle, but in horses, and"—adjusting the reins—"I've been blessed in so many ways I can't count. You're right. Satish's foals will be the future of this ranch."

He nodded.

"Tell me, how's the wife and kids doing? And the new house plans coming?" Jill asked.

As they rode close to the fence line, Sam said, "Debbie is a real trouper. When she left the bright lights to come here and marry me, she had a lot of adjusting to do. I'm an outdoor man, work from sunup until sunset, and she was used to the fast office men, theater, opera, and first-class restaurants and hit movies. Our community is slow paced, but welcoming and tight. We have a museum, small family-owned theater, and now a new library. We have a strip of diners and fast food. But with her being a God-fearing woman, I was pleased when she joined our church group and began teaching the five-year-old class. Debbie is so talented. Maybe she'll go back to school and continue her education." He shifted in the saddle. "Through our two years together, it's been our faith that's carried us and our surprised twins that have counted. What blessings. Although those boys sure are a handful." His amber eyes twinkled and appeared warm. "With that said, I also appreciate Doug for the tiny house usage loan until our house is built. He's a good man, Jill." Sam laughed. "I thought when we first moved into the tiny house, it was tight, but now, with the boys, it's tough. However, Debbie makes it work, and in three months, our house should be completely built." He touched his hat. "We appreciate the land given us as a wedding gift and thanks for asking about the missus."

They rode a little further, stopped, and worked setting a fence post and that ended the range schedule for another day. Both mounted their horse, kicked its sides, and rode in quietness to the barn.

# Chapter 16

TARA WORKED THE Monday after Christmas in her office, keying files on the worming and shot records that Steve had left on her desk on the new beagle puppies. She took a moment and pulled out a folded paper from her purse and propped her fisted hand under her chin. She stared at the written letter from her landlord, blew out a breath, and read, "Miss Tara Scott, sorry to inform you, but I've made a business decision to place the White Road house property on the market the first of the year." What was she to do? Of course, she could sleep in her office, but what about her stuff? She wanted to scream or cry or throw something.

But she adjusted Steve's organized paperwork and began keying in again when thoughts flashed back to Theodor after the Christmas Eve event. She was still stunned; Theodor had outwardly displayed words of his affection toward her and asked her out on New Year's Eve. And then there were her uncle's words: "Poor man, give him a chance."

What happened to her uncle and his words to Theodor never to contact again? What changed and when?" Did she dare try again? Her cell phone jiggled, it was a text from Miss Tally. *Wow, this early, 6:00 a.m. Doesn't that woman ever rest?* she thought. Tara sighed. The text read: "Dear, thanks for the personal care given to our Theodor." She shook her head. *Our Theodor? Not likely ours.* She read on, "Your uncle has been a blessing also. I know from talking with Theodor he is grateful to be nursed to health and to be alive. With that put aside, well, there's too much for me to say, call me."

Tara said, "Call me? Like that's all I have to do. What about my life?" She tapped on the computer key, finishing the updates on the puppies. She huffed and puffed and decided to make coffee. Time now was 7:15 a.m. She waged war within herself for another ten minutes, sipped coffee, then finally said, "I'll make the call. After all, Miss Tally is up in years."

The ring was answered on first note. "Hello, Miss Tally speaking."

"Good morning, it's me, Tara Scott."

"Thanks for calling back. And let me get right to the point before we are interrupted. Theodor is a changed man in many ways. He's hired another financial/investor advisor and has turned the companies' travel for guest speaker and seminars over to Kevin. Theodor is semiretiring from his investment company."

Tara gasped. "He's what? Slowing down with work? Ha! I can't feature that. He lives for the next person, assignment, the thrill of success. It's his whole life. You should know his situation will only be temporary until—"

"Tara, Theodor is changed! Tsk-tsk, he's turned down all possible socialite engagements and dates. Tara, if I say this, please don't give me up." She kept tapping the computer keyboard.

"All right. You have my interest up, what?"

"Those women he dated or escorted around town, well, Theodor personally called each one and informed them he was off the market for good. I've been dealing with them and let's say Kevin is one happy man with Theodor's approval!"

A hushed Tara then whispered, "Why, Miss Tally?"

"I can only offer my personal advice. Tara, give you and Theodor time. Tsk-tsk, the phone lines are ringing off the hook. The clerks are late as usual, and Theodor just came in the office. Bye."

She glanced at her cell phone and hurriedly punched in number 1. It rang and went straight to voice message. "You've reached me. You know what to do," then it beeped.

"Uncle Doug, I need to talk with you, call me, or stop in. Miss and love you." Tara pocketed the cell phone and walked into the lobby area. She touched the receptionist's desk and wondered, *How can I feel so out of place in my own passionate business. It's a void, almost like a lost of someone or something.* She crossed her arms across her chest. Mary Beth came bustling in, signing, and saw Tara. She grabbed her in a hug. "About time you're here at work. We've missed you."

Steve appeared, hands in slack pockets, and nodded to Mary Beth in his swagger. He moseyed up to Tara, squaring his shoulders, and asked, "Are you back for good? Am I out of a job?"

Mary Beth dropped her handbag on the floor. She squeaked, "Is he unemployed?" The phone rang. Tara pointed. "Mary Beth, answer the phone." She turned and stared at Steve and said, "Come into my office."

He followed like a lamb. He closed the door behind him and waited to be seated.

"Have a seat, Steve. Would you like coffee, it's fresh."

"Black, please."

Tara poured, handed him a mug, and said, "Steve, your work is impeccable, and I thank you for asserting yourself at a time my uncle was taken out of the country and assisting me and covering for me when I was unavailable to be here at work." Still standing and tapping her nails. "Steve, business has definitely picked up, but I'm not sure if I can afford you your worth right now." Tara glanced at him.

He sat the cup down. "May I make a suggestion?" He waited for her to be seated.

"Go ahead."

"Tara, you've never asked, and I'm grateful. With that said, I'm a wealthy man. My parents own Johns & Johns Products, baby powder, skin lotion, wipes, among other things. I worked as a sales representative in my family's company for five years while attending college."

Tara paled. "Wow! That came as a surprise."

He scooted the chair closer. "I would like to co-own the shelter and be your pardoner. It has such great potential, boarding more animals, doing more adoptive fund-raisers, and specializing in guinea pigs and small critters. No one out there knows what you do in guinea pig's birthing. We can publish a care book on small critters and a doctoral issue on the delivery procedure that's not natural to the cavy. I can help with that!"

"I don't know what to say."

He stood, finished his coffee, then said, "Tara, think about my offer and let me know. Only don't take too long to make your decision." He walked from the office.

Tara finished the rest of the day without answering anyone's questions and muffled through the clinic until time to go home. She said, "Mary Beth, can you open tomorrow?"

Mary Beth glanced at Steve and said in high spirits, "Yes." Not waiting for him to reply on whether he would be bringing her to work, she asked, "What's up with you, Tara? Do you have to be somewhere?"

Tara locked the door and said, "I need to see to talk with Uncle Doug or Jill in the morning. I should be in by noon."

"Need a ride, Tara?" Steve locked hands with a wide-eyed Mary Beth.

"No, not tonight. Thanks though." She walked a block down the street and set in the clear plastic shelter waiting on the bus. Rain began; she buttoned her coat, clutched her purse, and felt the folded letter concerning her place of stay.

At the house, she was greeted by a wiggly Snow. "Come on, boy, out."

Snow batted his tail and pranced to the back door. She flipped on the outside light and opened the door. There was a chill in the air or was it just her. Tara switched on the fireplace and automatically rubbed her hands. She pulled out a TV dinner, placed it in the microwave, and let Snow in. "Hard day?" She scratched behind his ears and reached for his feeding bowl and then added fresh water into his gallon water jug. The microwave beeped.

Tara reached to turn on lights, but instead pulled her hand back and walked in the bathroom, drawing bathwater and adding smelly salts and bubble oils. She soaked in, hoping of freeing her mind on where to live, date or not with Theodor, or to copardoner. Her eyes flashed, opened to a pounding sound and doorbell ringing. Tara stepped from the claw-foot tub, grabbed her terry cloth robe, and scurried bare foot to the front door with a woofing Snow.

"I'm coming. I'm coming." She peeked out the little window; it was Uncle Doug. She opened the door, rubbing the crick in her neck. "Hello."

He blazed in and poured a cup of old coffee, flipping on the lights, mumbling, "Why's it so dark in here? You weren't in bed, were you?" He touched her forehead with the back of his hand. "You sick, girl?"

"No, not sick. And no, I wasn't in bed. The lights were off so I could enjoy the fire in the fireplace." She rolled her blue eyes. "What are you doing here?"

"I got your message. What's up?" He smiled as he removed his Stetson and unbuttoned his coat and said, "Jill picked up Miss Tally, and they went to the Ohio Theater for a new show. I won't see my honey until tomorrow evening. So"—after taking a sip of coffee—"did you take Theodor up on the date night for New Year's Eve?" He lifted his thick brows up and down and took another sip of coffee.

"No!" Tara screamed. "Why should I? Just because you and Miss Tally say so?" She punched the sofa pillow.

"Whoa, Tara," He wrapped his large arms around a shaking and an uncontrollable crying niece. "Shush, shush, it will be all right." Doug hugged her tight until she shed no more tears.

She stepped from his hold and hiccuped and with tear-streak face said, "Excuse me, I'll join you in the kitchen."

Doug searched for the tea bags; he knew Jill always drank tea when making hard decisions. He refilled his coffee and sat at the table, stretching out his long legs and crossing them at the socked ankles. He slid the tea to her. "Okay, now spell the beans. What's got you tie up in knots."

Tara handed him the letter from her landlord. He read, drank coffee, looked at her red-rimmed eyes, and said, "Tara, we can contact your landlord and see if he's willing to rent month by month until he sells this place." He paused then continued, "Girl, I have money. We can build you a place on your business land, or not." Doug watched her shake that stubborn redhead no. "Okay, we'll circle back to the landlord later. What else is on your mind?"

"It's Steve." She blew out a breath. "He wants to be a business pardoner, a co-owner in the animal shelter." She picked up and set the tea down. "He's got some great ideas, but I've invested so much to see my dream come true. Honestly, Uncle Doug, I'm not sure I want to share my livelihood."

Doug tilted his head and searched her blue eyes then reached for her hands, covering them with his. In almost a whisper, he said, "Tara girl, what's really wrong? I know it's not business. You're brilliant in that department just like your mom and dad. Talk with me."

Tara shifted. His grip tightened. "Okay, let me get this out in the open."

Doug was a calm and patient man; he sat and waited while humming a church tune "Trust and Obey." She eyed him and said, "I'm confused about Theodor. I heard what he said, but I listened to Jill and Miss Tally before, and we know where that got me. I was hurt and disappointed in him. You know. He let that woman dragged him away and kiss him and after he came to my house a few months ago, he kissed me like he meant it, and the next day, Theodor was in Aspen. I'm not sure he's really dependable for anything than one date." She rolled her eyes. "Uncle Doug, he's a playboy, a doomed bachelor of worldly ways. I'm well better off without him." She lifted a hand.

Doug said, "Tara, you know that stallion Satish was used to his freedom until a smart woman dealt for him. It took six months to build trust and get him to act on any commands. And that was time-consuming to build in the security he needed. But Satish was worth the trouble, and it's paid off. He's able to ride and be placed in shows and is quite a stud."

Tara glanced over at Doug. "What's all that got to do with Theodor?"

He chuckled. "Nothing, just wanted your mind to relax. Now take me."

Her eyes narrowed.

Hands held high in the air, Doug said, "I've dodged commitment and women wanton way all my life. Oh, I've had fun and experiences, but never anyone I wanted to hunker down with permanently until Jill. She is sweet, kind, trustworthy, hardworking, a great cook, and accepted me as I am, and she brought me back to the Lord." He paced the floor. "When she came to Aspen with the forms I needed and stayed to help me, not expecting anything in return and certainly not"—his face reddened—"not unless she was married and that kind of togetherness was never mentioned." He cleared his throat and continued, "I enjoyed our pure time together and truthfully, I didn't want another man to temp her. And when I realized she was the one, I purposed. Tara, I really didn't think she, a woman of her stature, could love me, but she does, and I'm happy and content. Best decision I've ever made, giving up bachelorhood. She's what makes me get up in the morning. And I thank God daily for her."

Tara clapped her hands and nodded.

Doug stared down at Tara. "I believe Theodor Welch met his match when he met you. Just so you know, he and I have had quite a few manly talks since his healing, and he's real about his feelings toward you. A man knows these things. Go to the dance with him. If you feel nothing or have any doubts about him, let that be the end of the two of you." He gave her a hug and shifted into his coat and boots. "Pray about him and think about what the two of you could build together if you only open your heart. I know that's scary. Been there."

"Uncle, thanks for coming over. Sure you don't want to spend the night what's left of it?"

Chuckling, he pulled up the coat collar and said, "Call me anytime. Night, Tara." He kissed her cheek and walked to his truck.

She cleared the cups from the table, rinsed them, unplugged the coffeemaker, and walked into her bedroom. She mused, *Doug made lots of sense*, but she yawned and climbed in bed. She heard Snow's tail swooshing and sleep came.

The sun was brightly shining through her window and Snow pranced. Tara slipped from the bed letting Snow outside, leaving the door open a crack while making coffee. Snow came in and nuzzled his cold nose against her. She lightly batted him away and said, "Go eat." She pushed the back door closed then poured a mug of black hot liquid and brought out her Bible. "Devotions and prayer is the answer to any dilemma."

An hour later, Tara needed to dress for work. She has peace but was still undecided about everything—the shelter, the house, and mostly rather to accept the New Year's Eve date with Theodor.

Mary Beth, always with a smile, glanced up when Tara walked through the door. The office was busy, and people were waiting with their animals to be seen. "Hi," she acknowledged, and Mary Beth grabbed the phone.

Tara nodded and kept walking into the clinic where she scrubbed her hands and placed on a lab coat. "Say, Steve, who's next?"

He pointed to the overhead pen notes and said, "Looks like Jill's Butch has been chasing squirrels again. He's over in the waiting area, nothing serious, but the scratches need washed out per your uncle, and his yearly shot is needed. Want me to look at him or do you want the beast?" He laughed for Butch was an oversized big fluff lapdog.

"I'll see to Butch." She moved in that direction, snapping on her gloves. She notified Mary Beth to call Jill and leave word for her or Doug to pick Butch up. Another wash snap of gloves and the six newly acquired adult cats were checked, tagged, and placed on the scheduled to be either spayed or neutered.

<hr>

Steve announced, "Whew. The office is empty. What a day."

Just then, Jill whisked in the clinic with Mary Beth close behind following her, saying, "Please sign Butch's release form, Miss Price, I mean Mrs. Symth," and tapping her board.

"Jill, how was the theater and Miss Tally?" Steve asked.

Jill abruptly stopped and said, "We had a wonderful time. The show brought back a lot of memories on our country's history. We ate at the Southern Hotel and then I took Miss Tally home and stayed over. Doug doesn't like me to drive at night in the snow." She giggled. "After all these years with me traveling up and down the roads in all kinds of situations and weather, I have a worry wart of a man, but he's a keeper."

Tara smiled and kept silent.

Jill said, "Tara, it's none of my business, but Miss Tally and I were talking, and she's convinced that Theodor is a changed man.

That he's notified the women of his life and placed an end to his wild ways. He only talks about you. Well enough said, where's my Butch boy?"

Tara momentarily left the room and brought Butch out to Jill. "See, he's really fine. Just a few scratches that we took care of, and he's had his yearly shot so he may sleep a little more. Uncle Doug was just making sure."

Jill scribbled her name across the form and handed it with the plastic card over to a waiting Mary Beth and said, "Oh, you naughty boy! Come here and let me love you."

Steve placed the lead on Butch and handed Jill the handle, all while walking them toward the front door. "Good night, Mrs. Symth, Butch." He handed him a cookie treat.

The overhead bell dinged. Tara locked the door and flipped the open sign over to the close sign. The three stared at each other. Steve said, "Mary Beth, do you want to stop at the pizza place?" And turning toward Tara, he asked, "Want to come along? Plenty of room."

"Sure, why not." Her stomach growled giving her away.

# Chapter 17

It was two days before New Year's Eve and still no word from Tara, Theodor stood in the ballroom at Studio 27, answering every one of Miss Tally's command. "Hang this. Lift this. Carry it over there. No, no, place the flooring over here."

He glanced at his cell phone again, not any text or calls. He heard, "Tsk-tsk, Theodor, send her some flowers and call Tara later tonight. Now move that fabric over by the window."

Finally, Theodor said, "Miss Tally, why didn't you hire people to do all this work. I want us to enjoy ourselves. And where is Kevin?"

"Here." Kevin came strolling in the room. "Miss Tally, at your request, I called the table company for their china, linen tablecloths, napkins, and added twenty-five extra chairs. The florist shop verified their delivery. And according to Miss June, Miss Tally, we need you to check with the catering company for their time of service. Oh, Miss Tally, Miss June wants me to let you know that the Jimmie Jazz five-piece band called and confirmed to being here on New Year's Eve, 7:00 p.m." He clapped Theodor on the back and festively said, "Thanks, Mr. Boss, for the referral in selected choice, single women." Raising his eyebrows, he asked, "Are you sure about the women?"

Theodor shuttered, "I am!" He walked away quickly punching in the florist's number. He waved at Miss Tally and left the building, drove his BMW to his townhouse, and parked then strolled inside. Flipping on the light switch, he noticed it was 8:00 p.m. Theodor inhaled and dialed Tara's number. Four rings went straight to voice mail. Great, he waited, recording. "Hello, this is Tara Scott. Leave a message, and I may get back to you." *Beep.*

"Tara, this is Theodor Welch, and I hope I haven't reached you at an inconvenient time. I've called to see if you have thought and perhaps considered my invitation for being my New Year's Eve date? I would like to hear from you as soon as possible." *Beep.* "Should I call her back? Was there anything else to say?" Theodor tossed his car keys on the coffee table and jammed his hand in his slack pocket. "Man, I didn't ask about the flowers or was I suppose to?" He walked into the kitchen to heat late leftover chili but made a peanut butter sandwich instead. "Where is my manly courage? I've never had any trouble connecting or sweet-talking any woman, that is, except for Tara Scott." Theodor paced the length of his townhouse. "Doug suggested that I be truthful on how I feel about her, face to face, and I did. Miss Tally employed me to send her flowers and call her, and I have. I've been a patient man." He poured a ginger ale and, after a cool sip, stated, "Most women would agree I'm a great catch, ruggedly handsome, neat, and I'm a clean person, stylishly dressed, money, charisma, educated, and know how to appreciate and show a woman a wonderful time. What's not to like or want?" His phone clicked. "Tara! She texted."

"Received the flowers. Daisies are my favorite, and the yellow rose mix was kind. Thank you. I've given your New Year's Eve date request much thought. And I accept your date night proposal. I'm not promising anything beyond New Year's Eve. If that's understood completely, text or call me with the detail plans, hum, you are quite the Fred Astaire on your feet. Your Ginger Rodgers for the evening, Tara."

"Wow, a thank-you and a compliment, but what if I mess up?" He toasted himself with the leftover ginger ale. "To us." Lifting high his arm, he then drank, emptying the glass. He smiled and belted, "At least she likes me."

The next day at work was like a zoo. His life became flooded with ghosts from his past. The available three regular women he escorted and had familiar happenings with the last eight years off and on came into his building. Miss Tally was straining, holding in her tsk-tsk. And Kevin was like a kid in a candy shop, staring at the exquisitely beautiful women. One by one each female was shown into Theodor's office, but only after being announced first and with an understanding. Miss Tally stayed in the room.

Jeanette Endecott was first to enter his office, a six-foot slender woman dressed in the finest navy-blue silk threads. She was sniffling. Miss Tally thumped the box of Kleenex in her hand and stepped back by the closed door. Theodor kept the massive desk between them and placed his spread hands on the desk. He was straightforward with his words.

"Jeanette, we've had our run and fun, but I'm no longer available. My life has taken a wonderful twist, I rededicated my life to the Lord, and I've found the most awesome pardoner." He left out if Tara would have him.

Miss Tally removed her lacy handkerchief from her dress sleeve and blew her nose.

Theodor pushed the main phone line. "Kevin, will you step in here."

An instant light knock wrapped on the door, and it was opened. Kevin nodded with smile to Miss Tally and searched Theodor's eyes. Theodor straightened, arms across his chest, and said, "Kevin, I would like you to meet Jeanette Endecott a…ah… an acquaintance. His face reddened. "Ms. Jeanette Endecott, this is Kevin Tillman, an equal associate of mine and a bachelor."

Kevin stretched his right hand out to greet her and said, "Hello, so nice to finally meet you." Eyeing her from head to toe and meeting her eyes, he smiled.

She moved closer to where he stood and asked, "Are you on the social market?" She fluttered her eyes.

With hands up in the air. "I assure you I'm a mover and a shaker."

She smiled and handed her business card to him and, at the now open door by Miss Tally, Jeanette paused and said, "Call me if you're lonely." Jeanette slithered out of the office and left the building.

Miss Tally pointed her index finger at a smiling Kevin. "Tsk-tsk."

He hunched his shoulders and walked to his desk.

Theodor exhaled and sat behind the computer, reading and answering client's e-mails that stated blessings, best wishes, and prayers for him. His office phone rang. He picked it up. It was Miss Tally. "Georgette Kim is here."

Theodor again stood behind his desk, Miss Tally at the office door, and Georgette entered in tears. He went through the motions, hands on desk, Miss Tally pushing the Kleenex box into Georgette's hand, and he stating, "Georgette, thank you for calling Miss Tally when I was in the ski accident. You know we've had our run and fun, but I'm no longer available, and I hear you've found quite the catch. My life has taken a wonderful twist. I rededicated my life to the Lord, and I've found the most awesome pardoner." He again left out if Tara would have him. "I'm off the dating market too."

Miss Tally still fluffed her handkerchief and dabbed her eyes. And Theodor pushed Kevin's extension, and he came in the office. Introductions were made, and Ms. Georgette Kim met Kevin Tillman. A hand met each other's and both walked together from Theodor's office with her talking about this new doctor and that she was engaged.

Miss Tally escorted Elisha Devin in to see Theodor, and the scene was much the same: woman in tears, box of Kleenex passed, Kevin stepped in, smiles, the two leave the office together, Kevin given a business card and told to call, and finally Theodor with headache still breathed a little easier.

Late afternoon, the newly hired associate, Gerald Sally, came in the office and met with Theodor. He was a man of medium built, height, and was married. Theodor welcomed him aboard and insisted he come to the company's party with wife even though officially his work assignments didn't begin for another two weeks.

That evening, Theodor took Miss Tally to Marcello's Restaurant and said, "Thank you, Miss Tally, for helping me become the person and businessman I am. You are a good Christian woman. You've must have prayed for me a lot." He chuckled. Then his black eyes narrowed. "Walking with God opens the door to wisdom and daily strength and the nerve to pursue Tara Scott."

Miss Tally nodded and said, "She's a great catch. Smart and pretty. I take it she accepted the New Year's Eve date?"

The waiter came, and they placed an order. "Yes, in a text last night. I did send her flowers, and I did call her only to leave a message on her cell phone, but she did respond. Yay me!"

Miss Tally said, "I know she's the one. Don't mess up, Theodor. Just pay attention to only her." She waited until the food was set down, and the waiter left. "Let her see the change in you. Theodor, you're a dear man."

The forks clunk, and the silence was welcome. The meal ended, and Miss Tally spoke, "One more thing, Theodor."

"Yes, Miss Tally?" he said, taking a sip of iced tea.

"So you're completely updated to the changes I made in the office while you were rehabilitating. I promoted number 1 clerk, June, to handle my regular hours as I've placed myself on your new part-time schedule." She patted her mouth with the linen napkin. "Theodor, Ms. June Fulton has proven herself to be loyal, skilled worthy, and puts the interest of your company first. She's a dedicated soul and is one to be reckoned with. Just between you and me, she'll keep Kevin in line."

With a chuckle, he said, "I understand, and I trust you with Miss June's placement." He smiled and continued, "I appreciated you staying on with me, well, putting up with me, but you do know I gave you quite a vast retirement package, stock in the company and a monthly salary whether you come in to work or not."

She fluffed her handkerchief again. "Tsk-tsk, Theodor, you are so thoughtful and kind to me. The retirement package was not a necessary, but thank you."

Theodor reached over and put his large hand over her two small bony hands and whispered, "You've been like a mother to me in so many ways." He rose, laid a stack of bills on the table, and came around to her chair and leaned in. "Miss Tally, besides Tara Scott, you're the only other woman I love."

She shook her head and tsk-tsk and stood walking arm in arm with him to the car. No words were spoken, just Theodor humming. He pulled up to her apartment, double-parked, and gently walked Miss Tally to her door and bid her a goodnight.

Theodor didn't go into the office the day of New Year's Eve but worked from home. At 4:00 p.m., he signed off work and happily sorted through his closet, selecting a black tuxedo. Now 4:45 p.m. and dressed, he texted, "Tara, my driver will arrive at your house 6:30 p.m. I'll be at Studio 27 front entrance waiting on you. I don't want Miss Tally handling the last-minute details by herself. Thank you again for accepting my date invitation, Your 'Fred Astaire,' forever, Theodor."

Miss Tally called, "Theodor, Kevin's bringing that Elisha Devin to the party. Tsk-tsk, you better warn Tara Scott of your past being present. Oh, the chairs are being unloaded. Must go."

Theodor entered the ballroom and what a difference a day made when Miss Tally was in charge. She greeted him,

"Handsome, you are bowtie and all," and handed him his New Year's Eve hat. "The noisemakers are in a basket at each table, self serve." Then Miss Tally walked over to Ms. June Fulton who appeared to be giving instructions to the guest.

The jazz band was setting up; some testing their instrument. Theodor saw he really wasn't needed. But as CEO, he stood in the archway greeting clients, meeting their significant other or date, and spoke to the staff as they entered in, keeping a close eye on the front door. He felt edgy waiting on Tara.

Kevin waltzed in with Elisha arm in arm. He, of course, in tuxedo and she dressed in a slinky rust-colored flair long dress, which swished as she walked. They paused, and she reached out her gloved hand. He put it to his lips and gave her gloved hand a kiss. She said, "Darling, I want a dance with you for old time's sake," giving a little wiggle and tilting her head back and sending a chilling laugh through the air.

Theodor's smile disappeared. He shifted on his feet and said, "There is no old time's sake. Enjoy your evening, Miss Devin." He clicked his feet, nodding to Kevin, and said, "Keep her in line!" and bolted to the front door as Tara walked in. Theodor's knees were weak, and his heart raced.

She smiled, and her blue eyes met his. She said, "Hi, Fred," and offered him her cloak.

Theodor just stood there unable to utter a word. He found himself ogling her. She was exquisitely breathtaking; he had never seen another woman with her beauty. And then her porcelain shapely leg appeared from the side slit in her long form-fitting creamy-white dress with gold and silver threads. He inhaled, and his mouth went dry like cotton. Finally, he reached out and received her wrap, bowed, and offered his arm and was surprised he could move. He seated her at their assigned table. And he was relieved when Miss Tally came by with hat in hand and offered it to Tara. Theodor said, "Excuse me, ladies, and I'll check in Tara's wrap." He turned then walked away.

Theodor realized he had been holding his breath and exhaled with quick intake. He pocketed the cloak number, stopped by the open bar, and selected two nonalcoholic bubbly flutes and set one down in front of Tara. She picked up the glass and lightly placed her full red lips on the edge of the glass. She tilted her head upward. "Theodor, are you setting?"

He gave a quick smile hoping his lips showed more than a growl, and sat sipping the bubbly. The music played. Theodor glanced in Tara's direction and said, "Care to dance with me, Ginger?"

She placed her hand in his. They walked on to the dance floor. Others were also dancing yet the dance floor was not crowded for people were still arriving. He bowed then offered her his hand while placing the other on her back. The waltz was awesome. She was close and in his arms and moved with him so easily. Her flowery fragrance wavered under his nose, and he pulled Tara closer and whispered, "I'm the luckiest man here. You are so gorgeous." He twirled and said, "Thank you for this night. I trust I prove myself worthy to you," and dipped her. Her lips were so near to his, and he felt their breath mingle. His shirt collar became too tight, and the desire to taste her cherry lips pulled him as if he were in water drowning. He saw her eyes flutter and her chin lift. Time stopped until he heard the clapping.

Tara's face was flushed. He bowed to the audience and upon raising, Elisha and Kevin stood by them. She ran a hand over the body of her dress and said, "Theodor, introduce me."

His carriage changed and his nostrils flared. Theodor knew; his arm tightened around Tara's. He felt sweat beads form on his forehead. He watched as if in slow motion. Tara's blue eyes brightened. She offered her hand to the other woman. Theodor felt doom.

Kevin cleared his throat and said, "My date, Elisha, meet Ms. Tara Scott." He glanced over at Theodor's eyebrows lifting and said, "Enjoy your evening, folks," and whisked away Elisha, whispering in her ear. Her shrill laughter filtered the room.

Theodor reached for both Tara's small hands; he leaned in. "I'm so sorry about—"

Tara on tiptoes said, only for his ears, "I know you have a pass and I see who she is with and I know who my date is, Fred." She slid her arm around his waist looking up at him, batting those blue eyes, and laughed.

"How did I get so blessed?" He kissed her cheek, and they danced to another slow-playing tune. When the dance ended, he escorted her to their table and waited to be served. He was surprised when, throughout the meal, she placed a hand on his arm or shoulder as an endearment. When they move and their thighs touch, electricity sizzled even through their clothes. His stomach rolled, and his appetite was gone. He was amazed that she could eat and make conversation with others at their table. He needed to gain control and thought, *Where are my charming ways?*

Tara sweetly asked, "You all right, Theodor?"

He nodded, running a finger around the shirt collar. He quietly gave himself a pep talk then turned toward her and said, "Tara, I know it's eleven fifteen and New Year's Eve is counting down, but if you wouldn't mind, I want to leave."

She placed her napkin on the plate, rose, and in a whisper said, "I'm sorry I disappointed you tonight." Tara turned to walk away.

Theodor muttered, "Shucks!" He waved to a passing Miss Tally and mouthed, *We're leaving*, and strode after Tara, calling out, "Please wait." He noticed her face was pasty as he caught her arm and whisked her aside, staring into her innocent blue eyes, and said, "For a man of my forthrightness, I was so terrible in saying what I didn't mean." He let out a breath. "Tara"—he touched her cheek—"I would like for you to attend the community church service tonight with me. They are having a New Year's Eve program. Well?"

Her mouth gaped and her eyes brightened and her grip on his arm was deadening. Theodor didn't look away; he was waiting, hoping, for her yes answer.

# Chapter 18

TARA WAVED TO everyone and shut the front door finally after encouraging the gang and Theodor to leave. The party went on and on; it was now 3:45 a.m., and she had to be up by seven, no, at work by 7:00 a.m. She was still pumped by the happenings and their suggestions and said, "How am I supposed to sleep with all the excitement and with the New Year buzz." Tara changed her clothes and cuddled with Snow on the sofa. She heard the fire crackle and her eyes fluttered. Her thoughts returned to just a few evenings earlier. She had taken Steve up on the offer of pizza with Mary Beth, and afterward, Steve had kindly dropped her off at her home where she was greeted by a woofing Snow and faced with suddenly feeling alone. She had let her beloved Saint Bernard out and filled his food bowl and added fresh cool water to his gallon jug. She had looked around the room and thought, Why not take down the Christmas decorations for tomorrow is New Year's Eve. She had heard Snow woofing and let him back in and made her a tea.

Tara yawned remembering: The fireplace was lit, and she settled down on the sofa, taking a sip of Camellia tea going over Doug's words, "Theodor's feelings for you are real," and Jill's repeated conversation with Miss Tally, "Theodor is a changed man, and the women he socialized with are in his past." Tara had reached for her cell phone and at that moment sent Theodor a text. She hadn't promise more than just the date on New Year's Eve. And suddenly, she had felt a tingle of anticipation and joy.

The next day, she had volunteered Mary Beth on another quick lunch shopping adventure. They went to Polaris Center for the newest women's clothing store and accessories. Mary Beth had drove's Steve's sport car, leaving him at the shelter's clinic, and Tara had chatted freely, "Mr. Dreamy, as you call him," rolling her eyes, "is supposed to be a changed person. He's had a reconnection with God per Jill and the grapevine, Miss Tally. Did I."

Mary Beth held out a hand, "Hold that thought, I have to get over." The cars whizzed past and with blinker, Mary Beth darted into the turn off lane. The radio played, lowly the car was parked, and the engine turned off. Mary Beth turned in her seat and said, "Tell me what?"

"Well"—unbuckling her seatbelt—"Doug came to the house, and we had a long talk. You know he spent a lot of time with Theodor, and he's convinced on his change, so…" Opening the door, she said, "Eek, I'm spending New Year's Eve with Theodor at Studio 27. That's tonight."

Mary Beth squealed, "Let shop!" Then she stopped on the parking lot, hands on hip, and her breath rolling out as she said, "Why do you always wait until the last minute."

Tara nudged Mary Beth and reached for her shoulder handbag. "Are you going to help me or not?"

Minutes later, Mary Beth held four evening dresses on her arm and said, "Try these on." She shook her head, bunching her mouth, until the last dress appeared on Tara.

"That's the one." She pointed at her. "Mr. Dreamy will drool."

Silver shoes were selected, no hoses per Mary Beth, and no jewelry. Cash was paid, and Mary Beth rushed Tara out the door. In the car, she made a call to Steve. "On our way back, can you hold down the fort a while longer? I need to help Tara with a project at her house."

"Sure, Mary Beth, be careful. If you're not back by closing, I'll catch a bus and meet you at Tara's house." Silence then *buzz, buzz.*

Time then was 4:35 p.m. Tara saw a miss text from Theodor. "Shoot, Mary Beth, Theodor is sending a car for me. The driver will pick me up at 6:30 p.m. How will I ever get my mop set and me dressed? And just look at the traffic."

Mary Beth switched the radio off and said, "Now would be a good time to pray, Tara, for safety and speed and for the driver to be late." She giggled.

At the house, Mary Beth had taken charge. "Grab a shower, use your flora-scented soap and lotion, wash your hair, and leave the rest up to me—go!" Mary Beth walked Snow out the door and lined the kitchen table with products from her purse—liquid makeup; rouge; eye shadows; blue, yellow, silver, white, and glitter; then mascara; hair jel; spray; and a paste.

It was then ten after six, and Mary Beth handed the portable mirror to Tara. "Well, what do you think?" She fluffed the red curls that dangled and sprayed them again.

Tara batted at the smoke of spray. "You're killing me!" She turned her face from one side to the other. "Mary Beth, don't you think my makeup is a little heavy?"

Mary Beth viewed the front and walked side by side. "Nope." She brought out her red lipstick and said, "Open your mouth. There. Let me help you slip on your dress."

Tara wiggled the dress down and pulled at the zipper. Mary Beth slapped her freshly painted nail hand and said, "Stand still. Zipper up, hold still." A squirt of perfume aired from head to toe, and she said, "Spread, um," tapping on her leg. Another spray upward. The doorbell had dinged. Mary Beth glanced out and smiled. It was Steve. She opened the door and waved him in. He leaned forward and lightly kissed her cheek and walked into the kitchen. "Well, hello, mademoiselle, and who are you? And what did you do with Tara?"

Tara giggled and slapped his shoulder. He was still watching. The doorbell dinged again, and it was Theodor's driver who called for Tara. Steve walked her to the door and said, "You're a beautiful woman inside and out. Have a great evening."

Tara had paused. "What's your and Mary Beth's plans this night to ring in the New Year?"

"Hopefully," he had said, "a quiet time, pizza, pop corn, movie, a few songs, and a devotional with my best girl, Mary Beth."

The driver's smile had deepened when Tara walked to the car. He'd opened the door, exposing the back seat, and said, "Miss, I don't mean to step out of line, but you're a breath of fresh air, and no one in Hollywood could hold a candle to you."

She'd slid in and waited until he closed the door and was behind the wheel. Then Tara tapped him on the shoulder and said, "Thank you for the compliment, and Happy New Year to you, sir."

The driver nodded and slid the glass partition close between them and pulled out onto the street. Upon arriving at Studio 27, the driver double-parked and came around and opened her door. Just then, a laughing Doug rounded the building dressed in a black tuxedo with his wife, Jill, dressed in a full floor-length taffeta blue strapless gown. Doug said, "My love, you should let me place your cloak around your lovely bare shoulders, dear, it's cold out here."

Jill smiled into his eyes, and Tara heard her say, "Cowboy, you'll keep me warm," and then winked. Jill didn't even see Tara in front of her. The Studio 27 door opened automatically and in Tara stepped. Theodor rallied over to her and just stood there gazing at her. He hadn't spoken, and he didn't seem to notice Doug or Jill as they walked by even though Doug slapped him of the back.

Tara finally broke the silence only after inhaling his manly cologne and checking him out from head to toe and meeting his black eyes. He was so masculine; his broad shoulders filled out his jacket and those narrow hip made her knees weak. She forced out, "Hi, Fred?" She reached for his arm that he offered. His black eyes carried a special sparkle, and his face wore a crazy grin. She thought of how jumbled her emotions were—a mix of happiness, joy, excitement, trust, doubt, and some fear. What if he found her uninteresting, not intelligent enough, or lack in some social savvy way; maybe she was even too common. But for the night, she willed herself to breathe easier for he was her Fred, and she was his Ginger. She smiled and felt her insides radiate like sunshine bursting in her soul.

Theodor had been quiet yet very attentive and comfortable to be around. He seated her and had stood up to one life ghost woman from the past and listened to Miss Tally and politely excused himself with her wrap and brought her a nonalcoholic bubbly. His demure manner appeared romantic and kind. He asked, "Care to dance," and properly placed his hands. And then the air, the man, the hold, the kiss; she couldn't bear the lost. His final words, "I want to leave."

Her world came crushing in on her. The anxiety of rejection caused a skip beat to her heart. She managed a few heavy steps away, but Theodor reached for her arm and sincerely apologized, saying, "About leaving, I wanted us to leave together, and I'm asking you to attend the New Year's Eve church service at 'Memorial Friends' instead of us staying at the company's party."

She searched his dark eyes and saw tenderness. Tara on tiptoe kissed his cheek and whispered, "I would love to go with you."

Again, his black eyes held a sparkle.

She said, "Aren't we a wee bit overdressed?"

He chuckled and said, "So?"

He was a temping challenge. Arm in arm, they waited for her cloak and then rushed to the car. He whispered something to the driver; he smiled and nodded. The keys were handed over to Theodor, and he opened the passenger side for her. He slid behind the wheel and the engine purred.

Time was 11:35 p.m.; he parked and hurriedly opened her car door and said, "Can you pick up the hem of your dress, we need to literally run." Laughingly, they skipped up the steps and were surprised when the heavy metal door opened for them.

"Good evening," the suited man said. "Here's a bulletin, follow me."

Tara slid her hands briefly over her tight dress and grabbed Theodor's hand. He pulled her with his large steps. They were seated midway up the aisle and a tune was being played by a violinist. It ended, and a trio of young ladies sang without aid of instruments. Their voices surrounded the large auditorium. Tara quickly glanced at Theodor, and he was engrossed. He reached over and linked their fingers together. A man stepped forward on the platform and asked each person to move to the front and take a candle. They followed the row in front of them and stood. The man stepped down carrying a box of candles and said, "Take one." A younger boy, most likely his son, followed with live fire on a small torch so mankind could light their candles. It was beautiful. The people lined made a complete circle with light.

The man said, "Each man, woman, boy, girl, young adult, pray a short sentence prayer as you feel led of thanks, praise, or hope representing the past year and to ring in the New Year. Don't be shy."

Theodor squeezed Tara's hand; he cleared his throat and praise words fell from his mouth, "Thank you, Lord, for saving a soul like mine."

There were a chorus of amens, and someone else spoke. No one hurried, and sniffles were heard, nose blowing, but a serenity, joy, and peace hovered the room. The woman next to her finished, and Tara found herself speaking, "Thank you for the gifts of work, friends, forgiveness, and love."

The gentle leading man said, "Blow out the candles, put them in the box, and all hold hands." He began singing "Bless Be the Tie that Binds."

People belted out the old, old song and then sang "Auld Lang Syne." The lights came up, and people shuffled to their former seats, picked up their Bible, purses, sweaters, coats, or jackets, and joyously bid one another a blessed and happy new year and left the church. In the car, Tara said, "Thank you for including me. I was touched and perhaps drawn a little closer to Him and you." She shyly glanced up at him.

Theodor started the engine and sat. "You're truly welcome, and I'm glad we could share this time together." His hands still gripping the steering wheel, he said, "Tara, Doug told me of your landlord's decision to sell your house and the offer of Steve's potential investment into the shelter." He held up a hand. "Hear me out, please. Doug didn't speak out of turn. We are genuine friends, and we share lots of stuff. However, my point is"—he searched her blue eyes—"Tara, I've fallen for you hook, line, and sinker. I want to be with you and no one else. Before you say anything, no, it's not gratitude I feel for you."

He began perspiring, cracked a window, and reached into his inside coat pocket. Then he opened his door and came around to her side and opened her car door and dropped on one knee in the snow. He looked up and said, "I know this seems sudden, it's not. So you know, I was attracted to you the moment we first met. And was convinced of that fact when you missed your bus and I took you home and you tenderly kissed my cheek. Oh, I know what I've said about bachelorhood and how stupid of me to think I ever enjoyed being single. But I didn't realize that fact until… after I met you."

"Shut up, Theodor. Quit babbling. What are you doing in the snow on your knee in a deserted parking lot with me? And going on about you and Doug's conversations." She giggled, shaking her head.

He reached for her hand but didn't get up. He said, "Tara, I love you with all my heart, and with God's help, I want to spend the rest of my live with you. If you'll have me, what do you say?"

He flipped open the black velvet box and lifted it, revealing a round diamond set in platinum and white gold.

The snow began falling again, and Tara's blue eyes locked on Theodor's smoldering black eyes. She was sure of her feelings for Theodor Welch. She loved him but answered, "Give me a moment." Tara turned from him and held her cell phone then set it aside. She reached in the glove box, turned facing the outside and Theodor, and handed him his cell phone. "I think you should check your phone." She set there perched watching him with her hands folded in her lap.

Theodor had wretched his eyes from her and glanced at his cell phone and broke into laughter, tilting his head. Text from Tara.

"Are you really Theodor Welch, my mistaken Internet man, my patient, my 'Fred Astaire'? If so, my answer to your proposal is yes, I'll marry you. I knew you were the one for me the minute I looked up and saw your intriguing black eyes staring back at me in front of Marcello Restaurant."

As he glanced up, she stretched her left hand out the open door and wiggled her ring finger. Chuckling, he placed the ring on her finger, rose, and leaned in for a kiss and lingered. He lifted his head, and she pulled him down to meet his lips again then said, "I Love your kisses. Now close my door, come around the car, get in, start the engine, and warm us up."

"Yes, ma'am." Still chuckling after sliding behind the wheel, he said, "And to think I thought you were shy." He started the engine and leaned over. "Happy New Year, darling." He gave her another lingering kiss and asked, "Where to?"

"Theodor, my house, of course."

He drove slowly not because of falling snow or the weaving drivers who had partied too much, but the thought of being separated from her a second was too long. He said, "When is our big day?" taking a hand off the steering wheel and entwining his fingers with hers.

She remained silent until he parked the car in front of her house and said, "Leave the engine run, please. We have a lot of things to figure out. Me, should I venture in business with Steve, do I want to expand the animal shelter business, and"—squeezing his hand—"where to live? I know not here." She pointed toward the house. "And surely not in your bachelor's pad townhouse!"

He placed an arm around her and kissed her quick. "Well, one idea, why don't we have a home built to the far side of the shelter over by the creek. There's plenty of land, yes? And our house could be built within four months. Tara, I have plenty of money."

Tara nodded and kissed him back. She opened her door and said, "I want us to marry soon." Her neck to face went red.

"Tomorrow would be fine with me." He glanced her way. "Or the day after. Big or small ceremony doesn't matter to me as long as it's with you. Seriously, if you want, we can marry in our house after it's built." Then with eyebrows lifting, he said, "We can honeymoon anywhere in the world you chose." He wrapped her in his arms and dropped little kisses on her cheek. "Between Miss Tally, Kevin, Jill, and your uncle Doug, Steve, and Mary Beth, our businesses and everything else would be well cared for. Besides, we'd only be a jet away."

"Oh my, you take my breath away. You sure were slow making your decision in forsaking bachelor lifestyle and now you're heading for a train wreck moving forward. So, whoa, let just say we enjoy our courtship, however long or short we choose, settle in to a church, ask for God's guidance on our personal and business life." Quick kiss. "I do like the ideas of our house being built on the land with the shelter and our marriage there in four months. But tomorrow will be another day. Let's think things over and meet with a clearer head. Walk me to the door, Theodor."

At the door, he lingered and said, "Wait until Miss Tally hears about us." Just then, the outside light came on, the door opened, and the whole gang—Mary Beth, Steve, Jill, Doug, and Miss Tally—stood in the open doorway, yelling, "Surprise and congratulations."

Doug stepped forward and said, "About time you got out of the car. I thought I was going to have to come out after you."

Miss Tally reached around Doug for Theodor's arm and tugged him and Tara inside, hugging them. Theodor looked at Tara and whispered, "How did they know?" Then he glanced down at her hand and saw the cell phone and busted out laughing. "You and your texting." He swung her and said, "Well, all right." He lifted her left hand sporting off the ring finger. "Show everyone your ring so they'll know for sure we're engaged and it's official." Shaking his head, he chuckled.

# Chapter 19

Tara couldn't sleep. Everyone including Theodor had finally left. It was 3:30 a.m. and the beginning of the New Year workday. She patted in to the bathroom and a woofing Snow needed to go out. Tara finished off the coffee, black, and let Snow in. He lied on the floor, whished his tail, and slid back in sleep. However, her mind raced, and she was bubbling over from the surprised engagement proposal from Theodor. She took a shower and said, "I'll lie down for just an hour." She willed her eyes closed. The doorbell dinged, and Tara jerked. It was 5:00 a.m. Tara had slept a good hour. The doorbell dinged again. "I'm coming," She stumbled to the door, and in opening it, she screeched, "Mary Beth?"

She was clapping her hands and said, "Can I come inside? Tara, I just couldn't sleep! I'm so happy about you and Mr. Dreamy. Have you set a wedding date?"

Yawningly, Tara said, "Not exactly, but would you be my maid of honor?"

Mary Beth's eyes widened. They both hug. She said, "Yes, and let's make a fresh pot of coffee, add an extra scoop."

Sitting at the kitchen table, Mary Beth questioned, "What's the wedding details so far?" She tapped her long salon-tapered nails.

Tara sipped several times. "Theodor and I decided to build our home on the property on the west side of the shelter. According to him, it will take only four months. So that's where we'll marry."

"Oh, I'm so happy I can't stand it." Mary Beth sipped her coffee then added, "You know Miss Tally and Jill and your uncle will be so involved."

"Oh, I know, but"—Tara placed her hands on Mary Beth's shoulders—"I have you to run interference." They giggled. A smiling Tara said, "Come with me, Mary Beth." In her bedroom, she opened the closet door and brought down a large rectangular box. "This was my mother's wedding dress."

"Oh, it's classic, try it on, Tara. And here's the veil, hurry."

The doorbell dinged. "Who's coming to the house this early, it's only 6:00 a.m."

"I'll answer the door. Just keep on with the dress."

"Miss Tally?"

"Tsk-tsk, girl. I'm here to help with the wedding plans and Jill's on her way over. Theodor already called me at three and then at five thirty this morning. He wants me to speed up things for Tara and his wedding, stating he was meeting with the architect at 7:00 a.m. And Theodor had already confirmed the minister for their wedding." She walked into the bedroom. "My, my, Tara, what a beautiful Victorian picture you are and what a great fit. I wouldn't change a thing."

"As I told Mary Beth, it was my mother's wedding dress. I love all the lace, the pearls and diamond slivers that are designed throughout," Tara said.

"It's gorgeous." Miss Tally sat on the bed.

Tara turned. "Help me on with the veil, Mary Beth. And, Miss Tally, what's this about my wedding date?"

"Tsk-tsk, don't you worry your pretty little head about anything." She breathed and rushed the words, "The wedding date is set for May 6, in just four months. And we'll help add your furniture, drapes, and whatnots after you leave on honeymoon. As you know, the decorating team will completely take care of the inside and do decor outside for the wedding." Miss Tally fluffed out the veil, which flowed to the floor, and said, "Jill is going to swoon over your total look." She took Tara's hands in hers. "Now what I'm saying is Jill and I will make sure your house is totally ready for you when you both come back. Mary Beth has ideas and then there's Steve to run the animal shelter and will take care of Snow. Oh, his sloppy tongue." Miss Tally removed her handkerchief from her belt and tsk-tsk.

Mary Beth inserted, "Yes, I'll be here for Tara!" She glanced over at Tara where her open mouth had formed a perfect O.

Miss Tally said, "And to think all this mayhem came out of a text of who's who." Miss Tally snickered.

The doorbell dinged. "I'll get it." Mary Beth joined in on the laughter. "Hello, Jill, Tara and Miss Tally are in the bedroom." In between chuckles, she said, "Enter at your own risk."

Jill walked in to the kitchen, poured a cup of black coffee, and headed to the room with the cackling women. "Oh my, Tara, what a lovely vision you are." She stirred around in her purse. "Tara, here's something blue. It's a handmade handkerchief that belonged to my mother, and I carried it when I married your uncle Doug."

Tara's blue eyes teared.

Mary Beth said, "Now for something new." She reached in to her oversize purse. "Here's a necklace with matching teardrop pearls I just bought when we went shopping. It's my gift to you. Only let me borrow them back if there is ever my turn."

All eyebrows lifted.

Mary Beth helped slip off the wedding dress, and Miss Tally and Jill placed it in the long box back in the closet. Tara put on her everyday work cloths and blew out a breath. "Ladies, I had wished for a family, and I have all of you." Her cell phone vibrated. She said, "Text from Theodor."

The ladies set on the bed, and Tara quietly read, "Love, I've talked with the minister from Memorial Friends, and he has agreed to marry us after we meet with him and complete a six-week study about God's Word on man, woman, and marriage. Then we'll marry like you wanted in our home in four months. I can't wait any longer for you to be Mrs. Welch. The architect is breaking ground as early as next week. So after work, I'll meet up with you if it's all right, and we can walk off our home-building site. Your uncle is here with me and insists he be present to give some insight. Anyone you wish present is all right too."

Tara gazed up at the ladies, and in unison, all three said, "Me."

She reached for their hands and bowed in prayer, "Thank You, gracious Lord, for the man You've placed in my life and for these wonderful women." She squeezed their hands and continued, "May we always stay friends and search Your ways and acknowledge only Your path. Thank You for grace and mercy You bestow upon us. Amen."

The women gave a group hug.

Tara texted, "After work is fine. I love you, Theodor."

Mary Beth said, "You want a ride into work, Tara?"

Miss Tally said, "Jill, can you take me into town. I need to free up mine and Theodor's calendar for this New Year."

Mary Beth said, "Ladies, we need to plan a shopping day, hose shoes, our clothes, and"—batting her bright-green eyes—"and putting the wardrobe together for the honeymoon."

"Tsk-tsk. Say, what about a bachelorette party? You know Doug will do it up to the hilt with Theodor." She paused then continued, "Jill, let's figure out a guest list for the last wild night single's parties."

Jill hit her thigh and belted, "Yippy coyote. I'm going to enjoy this night. I didn't have a bachelorette party."

Everyone laughed.

Tara rode with Mary Beth in Steve's sports car to work. When they entered the shelter, Steve was talking on the shelter's phone. "Yes, we have beagle puppies, two male, two female." He rolled his eyes. "They're black, brown, and white. Some with more white, others with more brown, Mrs. Town, Debbie. You need to set an appointment so you could meet your bundle of joy. The puppies are full or vim and vigor. Wait a minute, here's Mary Beth." He held the receiver out and smiled at Tara.

Tara shook her head thinking, *Another day at the office*, and a giggle slipped. Steve caught up with Tara. He handed her a lab coat and said, "Best wishes on your engagement." A few steps away, in low whisper, he said, "Don't give Mary Beth any ideas."

Tara glanced in his direction and placed a hand over her heart. "I wouldn't think of it, Steve." She walked a little farther and washed hands and gloved up.

Steve lifted out a satiny long hair hamster and said, "The boy's mom thought it was a male when she made the purchase, but it's a she and about to have babies. Can you add three drops of vitamins in her water bottle?"

"On my way."

"And if there is a healthy male from the litter, we're to call the boy's mother." Steve placed the mom-to-be carefully in a glass aquarium and covered the top with a wire-inserted cover then watched the hamster. It scampered around the floor, scattering cedar shavings. The water bottle clang as it took a drink. When the hamster reached for dry food pellets using its front paws, the cheeks puff out. They were stuffed.

Tara made notes and updated the hamster's file. Next were the boarding dogs' outdoor exercise. Tara bundled and applied their leads. "Burr, hurry up!" She stomped her booted feet and clapped her gloved hands; she read the thermometer, twenty degrees.

Inside, the day passed quickly. Mary Beth and Steve had left the building, and Tara washed her hands at the end of the workday and put lotion on them. She heard his baritone voice, "Hello, Tara, you back here?" She shivered but not from being cold.

She met him with a smile. His black eyes glistened. Tara had never been so happy. He embraced her and said, "Today couldn't end quickly enough so I could see you." He bent, pulled her close, and kissed her soundly. As Tara gazed up into his beautiful black smoldering eyes, she saw the promise of all their dreams of today and hopes for tomorrows.

"Tara, bundle up. It's cold outside."

After buttoning her coat and slipping on her hat and gloves, she anchored her hand with his and anxiously walked the steps with him while Doug roped off the length and width of their future newly built home. They were in agreement with the architect. Jill, Mary Beth, and Miss Tally were cheering and adding in their two cents. Doug came to the blissful couple and motioned the ladies to join hands. He prayed, "May our friendships grow stronger and may we let You Lord always be our guide and walk with You."

Theodor added, "Thank you, Lord, for extended family and true friends."

A lot of amens from the women; then Doug turned and said, "To the happy couple, long life and many children!"

Miss Tally shook her head and said, "Tsk-tsk."

CPSIA information can be obtained
at www.ICGtesting.com
Printed in the USA
LVOW04s0521140816
500230LV00006B/20/P